CARIBBEAN WRITERS SERIES

33

Tales of the Wide Caribbean

GW00750229

Tales of the Wide Caribbean

Jean Rhys

Selected and introduced
by Kenneth Ramchand

HEINEMANN
LONDON · KINGSTON

Heinemann Educational Books Ltd
22 Bedford Square, London WC1B 3HH
PO Box 1028, Kingston, Jamaica

IBADAN   NAIROBI
EDINBURGH   MELBOURNE   AUCKLAND
SINGAPORE   HONG KONG   KUALA LUMPUR
NEW DELHI

Heinemann Educational Books Inc
70 Court Street, Portsmouth, New Hampshire 03801, USA
All stories by permission of André Deutsch except
Trio, Temps Perdi and Invitation to the Dance
© The Estate of the late Jean Rhys

British Library Cataloguing in Publication Data

Rhys, Jean
  Tales of the wide Caribbean: short stories.—
  (Caribbean writers series; 33)
  I. Title   II. Ramchand, Kenneth   III. Series
  813[F]   PR6035.H96

  ISBN 0–435–98749–6

Set in 10/11 pt Palatino by Activity Ltd, Salisbury, Wilts
Printed by Richard Clay (The Chaucer Press) Ltd, Bungay, Suffolk.

Contents

The Published Writings of Jean Rhys

Collections of short stories

The Left Bank and other stories (London: Jonathan Cape, 1927; New York: Arno Press, 1970) contains 'Illusion', 'A Spiritualist', 'From a French Prison', 'In a Café', 'Tout Montparnasse and a Lady', 'Mannequin', 'In the Luxemburg Gardens', 'Tea with an Artist', 'Trio', 'Mixing Cocktails', 'Again the Antilles', 'Hunger', 'Discourse of a Lady Standing a Dinner to a Down-and-out Friend', 'A Night', 'In the Rue de l'Arrivée', 'Learning to be a Mother', 'The Blue Bird', 'The Grey Day', 'The Sidi', 'At the Villa d'Or', 'La Grosse Fifi', 'Vienne'.

Tigers are Better Looking (London: André Deutsch, 1968; New York: Harper & Row, 1974) includes nine stories from *The Left Bank*, together with eight previously uncollected stories: 'Till September Petronella', 'The Day They Burned the Books', 'Let Them Call it Jazz', 'Tigers are Better Looking', 'Outside the Machine', 'The Lotus', 'A Solid House', 'The Sound of the River'.

Sleep It Off Lady (London: André Deutsch, 1976; New York: Harper & Row, 1976) contains 'Pioneers, Oh, Pioneers', 'Goodbye Marcus, Goodbye Rose', 'The Bishop's Feast', 'Heat', 'Fishy Waters', 'Overture and Beginners Please', 'Before the Deluge', 'On Not Shooting Sitting Birds', 'Kikimora', 'Night Out 1925', 'The Chevalier', 'The Insect World', 'Rapunzel, Rapunzel', 'Who Knows What's Up in the Attic?', 'Sleep It Off Lady', 'I Used to Live Here Once'.

Penguin Modern Stories (London: Penguin Books Ltd, 1969) includes two short stories by Jean Rhys: 'I Spy a Stranger' and 'Temps Perdi'

Other Published Writings

Postures, later known as *Quartet* (London: Chatto & Windus, 1928; New York: Simon & Schuster, 1929. Reissued as *Quartet*, London: André Deutsch, 1969; New York: Harper & Row, 1971)

After Leaving Mr Mackenzie (London: Jonathan Cape, 1930; New York: Alfred A. Knopf, 1931. Reissued London: André Deutsch; New York: Harper & Row, 1972)

Voyage in the Dark (London: Constable, 1934; New York: William Morrow, 1935. Reissued London: André Deutsch, 1969; New York: Harper & Row, 1972.)

Good Morning, Midnight (London: Constable, 1939; New York: Harper & Row, 1970. Reissued London: André Deutsch, 1967)

Wide Sargasso Sea (London: André Deutsch, 1966; New York: W. W. Norton, 1967)

My Day (New York: Frank Hallman, 1975) includes 'Invitation to the Dance'

Smile Please: An Unfinished Autobiography (London: André Deutsch, 1979; New York: Harper & Row, 1979)

Jean Rhys Letters, 1931–1966 (London: André Deutsch, 1984)

Introduction

This selection has been put together from material already published in *The Left Bank and Other Stories* (London: Jonathan Cape, 1927), *Tigers are Better Looking* (London: André Deutsch, 1968), *Sleep It Off Lady* (London: André Deutsch, 1976), the anthology *Penguin Modern Stories 1*, edited by Judith Burnley (London: Penguin Books Ltd, 1969); and a short autobiographical work, *My Day* (New York: Frank Hallman, 1975). There are one or two unpublished stories and versions of published ones in the Jean Rhys collection at the University of Tulsa, but these have not been considered for this gathering.

Two stories stand out from the rest in the first collection, *The Left Bank and Other Stories*, in that they have identifiably Caribbean settings, and recognizable Caribbean characters. 'Mixing Cocktails' is less a story than a sketch containing impressions: a house in the hills; a child absorbing melancholy influences from the mountains, or gazing wistfully down a green valley to the deepest loveliest sea, where the steamers pass to and from faraway places; a vague passive child, shrinking from a hypocritical and respectable English aunt and from the strictures of adults who want her to be just like other children; and at last, a partly self-pleased, partly ironic performer of a single meritorious action – the mixing of the nightly cocktail. In the second of the obviously Caribbean pieces, 'Again the Antilles', a distanced and affectionate first-person narrator describes a literary skirmish erupting in the *Dominica Herald and Leeward Islands Gazette* between the peppery Mr Hugh Musgrave, a seasoned planter of twenty years, and the coffee-coloured Papa Dom, firebrand editor of the paper, and pseudonymous inveigher against social evils in its letter pages. In short space, and with the lightest of touches,

Rhys evokes race and colour tensions between white Creole and coloureds, and pokes fun at the mimic colonial mentality.

None of the other stories in *The Left Bank* evokes landscape as sensuously as does 'Mixing Cocktails', and none can suggest so effectively, by gesture, tone, or descriptive phrase the sense of a society and its living past which comes out of 'Again the Antilles'. But here is Ford Madox Ford in the preface to Rhys' first collection: 'I tried...very hard to induce the author of *The Left Bank* to introduce some sort of topography of that region, bit by bit, into her sketches....But would she do it? No! With cold deliberation, once her attention was called to the matter, she eliminated even such two or three words of descriptive matter as had crept into her work.' In order to answer the imagined reader's questions 'Where did all this take place?' and 'What sort of places are these?' Ford gives over the greater part of his preface to a description of the Left Bank itself, supplying against his better instinct what the author had refused to deliver.

Yet Ford's offer to account for the difference between the Caribbean stories and the Paris ones is not satisfying: 'Her business was with passion, hardship, emotions: the locality in which these things are endured is immaterial.' The Paris stories have a social atmosphere and a sense of place sufficient to the fiction. But the short stories with an English setting, published in *Tigers are Better Looking* and *Sleep It Off Lady*, which are no less involved in 'passion, hardship, emotions', do gain in texture and in theme from the author's greater familiarity with London and England generally, or ideas of them. Surely, one of the factors influencing Jean Rhys' practice was that she had less insight into the workings of society in Paris or France, and was less affected by the landscape there than was the case with London and England. It becomes clearer and clearer from her writings that the impressions of the West Indies, formed earlier, were deeper and more lasting than her impressions of either France or England. Ford himself had stumbled onto this (and more, without knowing it) when he remarked that Rhys 'lets Montparnasse or London or Vienna go,' but hands you the Antilles, 'the effect of landscape on the emotions and passions of a child being so penetrative'.

It is as true of the Caribbean as of the non-Caribbean stories that interest seldom lies in the event itself or in the progression of intricate plot, and Rhys hardly ever extends a short story to the point where a reader might begin to wonder whether the adjective 'short' is really applicable. The success of 'Temps Perdi', a longish story in three parts, dealing with three different times and places, underlines the point that in nearly all the stories unity and structure are derived from strong personal feeling, the characteristically understated intensities being complicated by spontaneous symbolism, as in this description from 'Outside the Machine': 'There were fifteen beds in the tall narrow room. The walls were painted grey. The windows were long but high up, so that you could see only the topmost branches of the trees in the grounds outside. Through the glass the sky had no colour.' It is worth adding here however, that Rhys' natural symbolism works in the other direction sometimes, to modify the oppressive burden of a particular story, as in the following sentence from 'Temps Perdi' where indomitable spirit subsists: 'Everything has run wild, but there was still hibiscus growing by the stone garden walls and butterflies made love over the thorny bougainvillea.'

A description, in *Smile Please*, of the smaller of the two estates in her childhood, and Rhys' account of the pull of her native place allow us to identify the landscape as one of the early sources of the intense feeling and what one might call the lyric structure in her stories:

It was there, not in wild beautiful Bona Vista, that I began to feel I loved the land and to know that I would never forget it. There I would go for long walks alone. It's strange growing up in a very beautiful place and seeing that it is beautiful. It was alive, I was sure of it. Behind the bright colours the softness, the hills like clouds and the clouds like fantastic hills. There was something austere, sad, lost, all these things. I wanted to identify myself with it, to lose myself in it. (But it turned its head away, indifferent, and that broke my heart.)

The earth was like a magnet which pulled me and sometimes I came near it, this identification or annihilation that I longed for. Once, regardless of the ants, I lay down and kissed the earth and thought, 'Mine, mine.' I wanted to defend it from strangers. Why was I sure that in the end they would be defeated? They can't cut down the silent mountains or scoop up the eternal sea but they can do a lot. The trees and flowers they destroy will grow again and they will be forgotten.

To this landscape, with its sudden variations of light and shade, its quick cycles of efflorescence and rot, Rhys owes at least part of her sense of mutability in the world, her awareness of death, misfortune, poverty, disease: 'I had everything; my God, I had. Eyes, hair, teeth, figure, the whole damned thing. And what was the good of it?' asks Lotus Heath in 'The Lotus'. To it also, one might add, she owed her enduring sense of regeneration, and of the indestructibility of whatever is fragile and beautiful, however battered by 'strangers'.

In the stories with a Caribbean setting, sea and sky, forest and mountain, river and rock, and burning sun are given simply as elements that are there, a natural source of simile, metaphor and symbol; and a subjective phenomenon reflecting and paralleling the moods and feelings of characters, or just indifferent to them. The narrator in 'The Day They Burned the Books' says of Mr Sawyer's retreat/library: 'The blinds were always halfway down, and going in out of the sun was like stepping into a pool of brown-green water.' In 'Temps Perdi', the narrator points out that 'the wind was blowing heavy luminous clouds across the sky, tormenting the thin crooked coconut-palms on the slope of the hill opposite the verandah, so different from the straight, healthy glossy-green coconuts just round the corner of the road – tame trees, planted in rows to make copra', so that we almost prefer to be the exhilarated and free trees on the exposed slope. Later on in the same story, we have to remind ourselves that it is of the horses that the narrator says, they are 'so thin that every bone showed in their bodies and they had the morose obstinate expression which is the price of survival in hostile surroundings'.

The Caribbean stories are also enriched by the felt and cohering presence in them of a remembered social world. The brutality of this world, its busy gossip, its whisperings and its sanctimoniousness are suggested in 'Pioneers, Oh, Pioneers'. The uncanny tendency of its envy, malice and hatred to create unlikely alliances even across dividing lines can be seen at work in 'Fishy Waters', a tour de force of narration. Here Rhys conveys a wide range of social perspectives not just from the substance of what the characters say and think but through the exploitation of a number of ironically juxtaposed linguistic registers and styles, including the epistolary (personal correspondence and letters to the newspaper expressing different shades of opinion), newspaper reportage, a prisoner's statement, defending counsel's plea, a magistrate's summing up, and dialogue between a husband and wife.

Always in the Caribbean stories we are made aware of the divisions and tensions between colour, class and race in a society whose structure derives from the plantation model. The respectable gossip tries to come to terms with Mr Sawyer: 'He must have a private income people decided, but they never decided why he had chosen to settle in a place he didn't like and marry a coloured woman. Though a decent, respectable, nicely educated coloured woman, mind you.' Like the marriage of Margaret Verlieu in the Walcott poem, 'A Country Club Romance', the mixed marriages of Mr Sawyer in 'The Day They Burned the Books' and the novice Mr Ramage in 'Pioneers, Oh Pioneers' cannot last. In the stories set in the Caribbean we find the soil of the rumour, gossip, innuendo, hypocrisy and malice of which the Rhys heroine remains acutely conscious even in the non-Caribbean stories, as if these breathings inhabit the air on their own. Such breathings are exploited brilliantly in a story set in England, 'I Spy a Stranger' where it is turned into a sophisticated narrative method, and where the talked-about protagonist emerges only out of what people say about her.

The social framework in her island allows Rhys some uncharacteristic comedy. But if she can poke fun at the colonial mentality, she can also point more tragically at her protagonist's crisis of identity and placelessness showing in concrete ways the connection between that crisis and colonial education or conditioning. The narrating character in 'The Day They Burned the Books' is 'tired of learning and reciting poems in praise of daffodils', and she has awkward relations with 'the few "real" English boys and girls' she meets. A friend helps her to begin questioning:

It was Eddie with the pale blue eyes and straw-coloured hair – the living image of his father, though often as silent as his mother – who first infected me with doubts about 'home', meaning England. He would be so quiet when others who had never seen it – none of us had ever seen it – were talking about its delights, gesticulating freely as we talked – London, the beautiful, rosy-cheeked ladies, the theatres, the shops, the fog, the blazing coal fires in winter, the exotic food (whitebait eaten to the sound of violins) strawberries and cream – the word 'strawberries' always spoken with a guttural and throaty sound which we imagined to be the proper English pronunciation.

Not even in moments of greatest isolation do the characters in the Caribbean stories appear to exist in a social vacuum. Without making them seem any less peculiar, Rhys can evoke a sense of her characters' typicality by a turn of speech, by tone or descriptive phrase; and she gives recognizable body to main and subsidiary figures alike by showing them in some form of social interaction. Even in a late Caribbean story like 'Let Them Call it Jazz', Rhys' sense of West Indian character and speech has not deserted her. Selina Davis, a mulatto woman in London, comes over as a defiant and inviolable person to a large extent because the remarkable and convincing dialect in which Rhys allows Selina to do the telling is in itself a declaration of a living identity. Rhys' memory of the Caribbean, and of West Indian society and speech pattern, remained so strong in spite of such a long absence that the artist could always find what was needful, and nowhere more brilliantly than in this story about an outsider and underdog in a foreign land. The following remark by a writing character in 'The Lotus' is convenient: 'The memory I've got you wouldn't believe. Do you know I can remember things people have said to me ever so long ago? If I try I can hear the words and remember the voices saying them.'

The other Caribbean stories not set in the islands are also stories of exile. In 'On Not Shooting Sitting Birds' the protagonist is a colonial soon to be freed of one kind of illusion: 'Before I came to England I'd read many English novels and I imagined I knew all about the thoughts and tastes of various sorts of English people.' While describing a fictitious shooting party to a young man she has decided to distract, she is remembering one that did take place. As the story progresses, other childhood memories arise. In the opening paragraph there is a reflection on memory which may serve as a convenient epigraph concerning the making and the therapeutic outflowing of all the Caribbean stories:

> There is no control over memory. Quite soon you find yourself being vague about an event which seemed so important at the time you thought you'd never forget it. Or unable to recall the face of someone whom you could have sworn was there for ever. On the other hand, trivial and meaningless memories may stay with you for life. I can still shut my eyes and see Victoria grinding coffee on the pantry steps, the glass bookcase and the books in it, my father's pipe-rack, the leaves of the sandbox tree, the wallpaper of the bedroom in some shabby hotel, the hairdresser in Antibes.

In another exile story, the narrating character tries to console herself with memories of home:

> But I was astonished to discover how patchy, vague and uncertain my memory had become. I had forgotten so much so soon. I remembered the stars, but not the moon. It was a different moon but different in what way? I didn't know. I remembered the shadows of trees more clearly than the trees, the sound of rain but not the sound of my mother's voice. Not really. I remembered the smell of dust and heat, the coolness of ferns but not the scent of any of the flowers. As for the mountains, the hills and the sea, they were not only thousands of miles away, they were years away.

The passage itself intimates that the 'so much that has been forgotten so soon' has not really been forgotten, and as we shall see, the Caribbean stories tell a tale of the phenomenal return of mountain, hill and sea.

'Overture and Beginners Please', the source of the last quotation, runs close to Rhys' autobiography *Smile Please* (London: André Deutsch, 1979), and describes the arrival and trauma of a young girl in England (at one point she is to be found reading a book called *The Dove in the Eagle's Nest*); unable to get warm, threatened by hostile streets, 'squashed up against perfect strangers', losing belief in herself but unwilling to accept diminished prospects ('The sky was the colour of no hope, but they don't notice it, they are used to it, they expect me to grow used to it'), and assailed by despair ('Despair, grey-yellow like their sky. I stayed by the window in the cold thinking "What is going to become of me? Why am I here at all?"'). In this rich overture are to be found many of the recurrent Rhys motifs – the concern about money; the use of snatches of verse and titles of books; the preoccupation with ageing; the fate of women and the cruelty of women to women; and the pretty dress whose absence or whose withholding by an unfeeling sales person can shatter the fragile ego.

Miss Born is only the first of a despised type (including, notably, Miss Bruce in 'Illusion' and Miss Spearman in 'A Solid House') representing breeding, culture and repression. Rhys's resentment of authority, respectability, and a colourless but lethal English attitude to life appears in different formulations throughout her writings. The protagonist in 'The Insect World', given as someone five years in London, terrifies herself with a book called *Nothing So Blue* (the actual title of a book by Elma Napier, another writer with Dominican associations) in which she reads about surly natives and tropical pests including 'the rats, snakes and poisonous spiders, scorpions, centipedes, millions of termites in their earth-coloured nests…the minute crawling unseen things that got at you as you walked along harmlessly' and the sand-fleas, jiggers that got in 'under your skin when you didn't know it and laid eggs inside you'. In this story, England becomes an insidious infecting world of insects, its regulated hordes hurrying along covered ways that peter out and lead to nothing, its swarms in the underground clinging to the sides of escalators. To Audrey there is no difference between the English and termites: 'They have railways. Tubes, bridges, soldiers, wars, everything we have. And they have big cities, and smaller cities with roads going from one to another. Most of them are what they call workers. They never fly because they've lost their wings and they never make love either. They're just workers.'

In 'Till September Petronella', the heroine's nostalgia for a long lost 'feeling of happiness, the fish-in-water feeling' and her admiration for Estelle the French girl, living in the same dangerous city, but who walked 'the tightrope so beautifully, not even knowing she was walking it', point to the wretchedness diagnosed by Marston: '"You poor devil of a female, female, female, in a country where females are only tolerated at best! What's going to become of you, Miss Petronella Gray, living in a bed-sitting room in Torrington Square, with no money, no background and no nous…Is Petronella your real name?"'. Anna in 'Mannequin' and the narrator in 'A Night' saying 'the Litany to the Blessed Virgin which I learnt at the Convent and have never forgotten', are continuations of the doleful exile figure: 'Mater Dolorosa: Mother most sorrowful. Pray for us, Star of the Sea. Mother most pitiful, pray for us.' To those acquainted with Rhys' fiction the hypocrisy, malice and ill-treatment experienced by the Rhys heroine, and her suicidal urges in the civilized dark she has voyaged in, are summed up by the young narrator in 'Overture and Beginners Please', demonstrating what she has learnt at the drama school: '"When you're stabbed in the back you fall like this, and when you're stabbed in front you fall like this, but if you stab yourself you fall differently. Like this"'.

The exiled person reappears in the vignette 'Trio' where a first-person narrating voice describes the increasingly sensuous and irrepressible behaviour of a young Martiniquan girl in the charge of a man and woman from her country. The narrator's growing involvement is signalled by the repetition of the phrase 'From the Antilles' (para. 2 and para. 4) until homesickness breaks the narrating stance in the final paragraph with this coda: 'It was because these were my compatriots that in that Montparnasse restaurant I remembered the Antilles.' In none of the other Left Bank stories does narrator or author declare herself so directly to be a child of the Caribbean; instead we find either that the third-person narrating perspective is that of somebody with a social conditioning unlike that of the other personages (a source of irony), or we encounter the odd main character who does not quite belong. Yet Rhys is unable to repress, or is unwilling to eliminate, elements associated with the Caribbean, a phenomenon even more readily observable in the English stories of *Tigers are Better Looking* and *Sleep It Off Lady*.

In 'Tigers are Better Looking', Mr Severn notices a girl 'with a really glittering smile and an accent he didn't quite recognise', a disdainful creature, debonair 'and with a touch of the tarbrush too...'; in addition to the white West Indian, Heather, Rhys introduces a mulatto playing the saxophone, and a 'lovely dark brown couple' the female half of which snubs Mr Severn 'with the most perfect British accent'. In the Paris stories, the author floats in Black characters (there is an Arab variant in 'The Sidi') to suggest warmth, beauty, spontaneity, emotional health, life – in short all the negritude qualities Anna Morgan contrasts with whiteness in the novel *Voyage in the Dark* (London: Constable, 1934): 'Being black is warm and gay, being white is cold and sad.' So in a corner of the Café du Dôme (in 'The Blue Bird') 'to redeem humanity sat one lovely creature, her face framed by a silver turban. Wisps of woolly hair peeped out from beneath it...'; and at the end of 'Illusion' a 'plump dark girl' gazing into the eyes of 'her dark plump escort' is used to concentrate the story's irony upon Miss Bruce. 'One thought of her', the deadly narrator tells us, 'as a shining example of what character and training – British character and training – can do. After seven years in Paris she appeared utterly untouched, utterly unaffected, by anything hectic, slightly exotic or unwholesome'. By the end of 'Illusion' the narrator has been enabled to see through 'the cool sensible, tidy English outside' to the yearnings for love and beauty in Miss Bruce's soul. The big square solid dark wardrobe opens to reveal a fabulous collection of dresses, colours and scents with which Miss Bruce secretly indulges her cravings at night, only to lock them up and return to solid square coats and skirts next morning. The return of the incorrigibly clean, calm and sensible Miss Bruce is marked by her constipated observation of the loving couple '"Not bad hands and arms, that girl"'. In this story about repression—not daring to disturb the flat sensible universe—and the stifling of life and beauty (a veritable anatomy of destructiveness and self-destructiveness), another Caribbean element appears in the form of a simile, to drive home the implacability of the Bruce imposture: 'She just looked at her surroundings in her healthy, sensible way, and then dismissed them from her thoughts....rather like some sturdy rock with impotent blue waves washing round it'.

There are other notable instances of Caribbean imagery as in 'At the Villa D'Or' where Mr Valentine the capitalist about to make a pass at Sara is 'like some cheerful insect with long, thin legs' (a singing mosquito). In the same story, Sara thinks of the voluptuousness of giving oneself up to that 'blue jewel of a sea' whose faint sound she strains her ears to hear. This sea-con-sciousness of the Caribbean writer returns again in the story 'In the Rue De L'Arrivée' in the description, after her fifth brandy, of Dorothy Dufreyne, 'a tiny shrinking thing in a vast, empty space', over whom 'flowed red waves of despair, black waves of fatigue, as the brandy crept warmly and treacher-ously to her brain. Waves from a tremendous, booming sea. And each one would submerge her and then retreat, leaving her dazed, and as it were, gasping.'

But while it can be argued that in the Paris stories Caribbean elements manifest themselves almost automatically as func-tions of the author's West Indian sensibility, the case is somewhat different in the English stories that come later. Here, the peripheral but normative Black is less in evidence and the Caribbean fragments belong to the memories of protagonists who seem to be based fairly directly upon the author at different stages in her life.

These memories are usually vague and nostalgic, and occur at moments of pain: Theresa in 'A Solid House' remembers playing hide-and-seek long ago in a cellar very like the one she takes shelter in during the blitz; and as the story unfolds, the solid house where she now lives, shows itself to be less and less of a refuge than that other one in the past, with its power to heal: 'The lawn was dark green and smooth and in the middle was a cedar tree. The rocking-horse under it was painted white with red spots. There wasn't a sound. And I knew that if I could pass the statues and touch the tree and walk into the house, I would be well again. But they wouldn't let me do that, the simple thing that always makes you well.' In 'The Sound of the River', a story in which Rhys' persistent memory of the sound of running water in her native Dominica plays a transferred role, there is a concentration in memory of a number of scenes that press on a sense of maternal depriva-tion: '(You're not my daughter if you're afraid of a horse. You're not my daughter if you're afraid of being seasick.

You're not my daughter if you're afraid of the shape of a hill, or the moon when it is growing old. In fact you're not my daughter.)' The childhood memory with which 'Rapunzel, Rapunzel' closes is West Indian but is not as easily placed as the convent memory ('sitting at a desk in the sun copying proverbs into a ruled book') of Miss Verney in 'Sleep It Off Lady'. Finally, the semi-recluse in 'Who Knows What's Up in the Attic' experiences an unusually hot day in the English countryside ('the sun was real sun, and the light gold') and feels 'as if she were in another time, another place, another country'.

An attempt has been made to show that in different ways the Paris stories and those set in England are not free of elements suggesting the penetrating effects of the Caribbean landscape and West Indian social experience upon Jean Rhys as a child. These fragments are brought closer in some of the English stories where an older protagonist's memory isolates a significant moment from a long ago period and a distant place identifiable as the childhood period in a tropical island. No figuring out is necessary in the case of the Caribbean stories whose subject matter seems to be the effects of landscape and social experience upon a child in an island. A child figure or a childhood memory occurs in all but five of the Caribbean stories. In one group of five, children are the protagonists; in three of them, a young woman remembers part of her childhood experience, while in another two ('The Bishop's Feast' and 'Invitation to the Dance') a narrator of advanced years looks back with the eyes of experience at particular occurrences in her childhood. A child, or children, separate from, or other than, the protagonist can be counted in another five of the Caribbean stories. In 'La Grosse Fifi' there is a highly significant episode in which a child-like young woman called Roseau, wrapped close in a flannel dressing gown by her ample and comforting friend, Fifi, 'mistily imagined that she was a child again and that this was a large protecting person who would sit there till she slept'.

The Caribbean stories with child protagonists include 'Mixing Cocktails', 'Heat', 'The Day They Burned the Books', 'Pioneers, Oh, Pioneers' and 'Goodbye Marcus, Goodbye Rose'. These are worth looking at for a moment. If 'Fishy

Waters', 'The Bishop's Feast' and 'Again the Antilles' provide a portrait of a social world, the stories with child protagonists lay emphasis on the effects of such a world upon a child, and they come over with much greater intensity than the three just mentioned, in which there is a distancing effect. In the group with child protagonists, the socializing process is seen as a force threatening the freedom of the child to be herself; adults, including the mother, are shown as harsh, uncaring, and quick to blame or misunderstand; the young person is withdrawn and burdened with hostile or distrustful feelings against 'humanity' and 'Other People'.

The girl in 'Mixing Cocktails' dares not laugh at her English aunt nodding in the unaccustomed heat, and a possibly too-indulgent author allows her to drift into being sorry for herself: 'I should like to laugh at her, but I am a well-behaved little girl...Too well-behaved....I long to be like Other People! The extraordinary, ungetatable, oddly cruel Other People, with their way of wantonly hurting and then accusing you of being thin-skinned, sulky, vindictive or ridiculous. All because a hurt and puzzled little girl has retired into her shell.' Mr Ramage in 'Pioneers, Oh, Pioneers' becomes for his individuality the object of white gossip and Black ridicule and is harassed into greater and greater eccentricity until he is murdered or driven to suicide. The child Rosalie weeps for 'My dear darling Mr Ramage' and writes the dead man a letter which is crumpled up and thrown out by a frowning mother. 'Goodbye Marcus, Goodbye Rose' presents loss of innocence in a social and domestic context which can provide no relief. The twelve-year-old Phoebe is too afraid of her mother to confide in her about Captain Cardew's obscenities; she has an oppressive conviction that 'no one would believe exactly how it had happened, and whether they believed her or not she would be blamed'. Repelled and fascinated by the Captain, no-one she knows can help her over her confusion, and all that she has been taught can only rouse a sense of guilt and personal unworthiness. Phoebe is sure that Captain Cardew had seen at once 'that she was not a good girl who would object – but a wicked one – who would listen. He must know. He knew. It was so.' The teaching of the Church also contributes to the child's sense of guilt, for 'didn't the nuns say that Charity in Thought, Word and Deed was your most precious possession?' In the bleak understated 'Heat', the child's prophetic vision ('there was no moon, no stars, but the edges of the cloud were flame-coloured') contrasts with society's vulgar reaction to catastrophe (gossip and a freak show), and the penitential narrating child knows there is no hope of explaining to 'Other People' that 'it wasn't like that, it wasn't like that at all'. The young girl in 'The Day They Burned the Books' sees too much of the race and colour tensions of her world too soon, and is exposed too young to maimed and spiteful adults nursing their rage and waiting for revenge. At the dark end, after the fire that consumes the books, the girl locks herself in her room to savour the title of a book she has salvaged, but 'it was in French and seemed dull. *Fort Comme Le Mort* it was called.'

These Caribbean stories describe a socialization process which induces the attitude in the child protagonists that parents, other adults, school, church and organized society work together to repress individuality, control and limit experience, abolish magic and dreaming, and make life safe, predictable and dull. The innocence lost in 'Goodbye Marcus, Goodbye Rose' was an innocence doomed to inauthentic existence anyway, and the narrative voice comes in to interpret Phoebe's withdrawal from the childish game of choosing a bridal trousseau and picking names for the babies to come as not being so bad after all. One can almost hear the author's voice encouraging us to recognize victory for Phoebe, since 'the prospect before her might be difficult and uncertain but it was far more exciting'.

The writing of a story is itself an act of fabrication, and the characters and situations in it are imagined or imaginary, so it is absurd to talk as if the facts in a fiction were the same kind of entity as the facts in a person's life. But the facts in the writer's life are the source of the fictional facts, and a critic cannot always do without reflecting upon the connection. The complexities in this subject did exercise and tempt Jean Rhys, and in the story, 'The Lotus', she allows a sinking middle-aged writer to recall some literary advice:

'That's what my friend told me,' Lotus said, ignoring her hostess. '"Whatever you do, don't be gloomy," he said, "because that gets on people's nerves. And don't write about anything you know, for then you get excited and say too much and that gets under their skins too. Make it up; use your imagination." And what about my book? That isn't sad, is it! I'm using my imagination. All the same I wish I could write down some of the things that have happened to me, just write them down straight, sad or not sad.'

Rhys' stories about childhood or those containing children assume special significance if we go carefully along with the commonsense inference, from pressure in the fiction itself, that there is a fairly direct connection between her actual experiences and the fictional shapings.

From the childhood stories, and from evidence in the autobiography *Smile Please*, it can be argued that Rhys was an acutely conscious and sensitive child, subject at an early age to an experience described compulsively in Chapter 12, Part Two of the novel, *After Leaving Mr. Mackenzie*. The chapter is given the title 'Childhood', and it occurs quite unexpectedly, with Rhys suspending the fiction in order to write an essay on an obviously pressing subject:

When you were a child, you put your hand on the trunk of a tree and you were comforted because you knew that the tree was alive – you felt its life when you touched it – and you knew that it was friendly to you, or at least not hostile. But of people you were always afraid.

When you are a child you are yourself and you know and see everything prophetically. And then suddenly something happens and you stop being yourself, you become what others force you to be. You lose your wisdom and your soul.

Technically, these are the thoughts of the character Julia, an embarrassing and down-and-out figure who, however, takes defiant pride in being a rebel against the socialization process. But the chapter is really a lament for the young human animal's loss of an instinctive mode:

No, of course you couldn't keep still. You were too happy, bursting with happiness. You ran as if you were flying, without feeling your feet. And all the time you ran, you were thinking, with a tight feeling in your throat: 'I'm happy –

happy – happy' – That was the last time you were really happy about nothing, and you remembered it perfectly well. How old were you? Ten? Eleven? Younger... yes,. probably younger.

The loss of this mode of being is associated with the birth of fear:

> And you could remember the first time you were afraid. You were walking along a long path, shadowed for some distance by trees. But at the end of the path was an open space and the glare of white sunlight. You were catching butterflies...
>
> That was the first time you were afraid of nothing – that day when you were catching butterflies – when you reached the patch of sunlight. You were not afraid in the shadow, but you were afraid in the sun.
>
> The sunlight was still, desolate, and arid. And you knew that something huge was just behind you. You ran. You fell and cut your knee. You got up and ran again, panting, your heart thumping, much too frightened to cry.
>
> But when you got home you cried. You cried for a long time; and you never told anybody why.
>
> The last time you were happy about nothing; the first time you were afraid about nothing. Which came first?

With the help of Ernest Becker's *The Denial of Death* (New York: The Free Press, 1973) it is possible to recognise the fear described in Rhys' novel as an instinct called fear of death, one that 'is natural and is present in everyone... the basic fear that influences all others, a fear from which no one is immune, no matter how disguised it may be'.

According to Becker, this fear is problematic. If it is too strongly present in our consciousness, it can paralyse us and make us abject. If it is allowed not to enter our consciousness, we become partly dead to the world, living a complacent existence as dictated by the socialization process. Rhys' rejection of the second of these modes is implicit in the sustained hostility in her fiction to the establishment. Throughout her fiction, on the other hand, there are debilitated figures on the verge of suicide or madness, helpless creatures, like Roseau, in need of comfort and swaddling and security offered by maternal figures or protectors, and baffled ones like Teresa in 'A Solid House', holding out against being 'normal' like the Miss Spearmans of the world, but paying a price. At one point Teresa seems to be ready for the easeful death of the Spearman condition:

> But are you telling me the real secret, how to be exactly like everybody else? Tell me, for I am sure you know. If it means being deaf, then I'll be deaf. And if it means being blind, then I'll be blind. I'm afraid of that road, Miss Spearman – the one that leads to madness and to death, they say. That's not true. It's longer than that. But it's a terrible road to put your feet on, and I'm not strong enough; let somebody else try it. I want to go back. Tell me how to get back; tell me what to do and I'll do it.

Rhys' heroines are proud in their rejection of the bourgeois and the conventional but are forced to be economically dependent. They despise complacent and insensitive people who are not alive to the risk and challenge of the human condition, but they are not able to suppress their consciousness of inevitable death for long enough intervals to be creative; their self-esteem, moreover, is too low to allow them to overcome their dark knowledge.

One cannot resist the feeling that the experience described in the childhood chapter of *After Leaving Mr. Mackenzie* is largely autobiographical. The coming of this experience to the child, Rhys, coincided with a number of social difficulties which it exacerbated, and which exacerbated it. Some arose from her growing consciousness of an unstable socio-political environment, and socialization in an unhealthy colonial climate similar to that described in the stories. Then there were unhappy experiences with her mother, with her foster-mother (the English aunt), and with the Black woman, Meta, described in *Smile Please* as 'my nurse and the terror of my life'. There are hints in unpublished sources of other traumatising experiences of a more sexual nature, but even without these it is possible to recognise that Rhys lacked what the psychoanalyst, Leon J. Saul calls 'inner sustainment', a sense of being well nourished and loved which tends to be founded upon good maternal experiences.

Rhys' removal from the scene of her unhappy experiences was also a removal from the setting that might have given her the nourishment to come to terms with those experiences. Her life and relationships in Europe were not such as to bring any kind of healing. And though she visited the West Indies in the 1930s she never returned there to live. But throughout her exile, the West Indies was on her mind. In the introduction to *Wide Sargasso Sea*, Francis Wyndham asserts that Rhys goes back in the novel to 'that spiritual country [the Caribbean] as to a distant dream: and discovers it for all its beauty ... to have been a nightmare.' It is possible, however, to trace a spiritual return of a more creative and liberating kind than that posited by Wyndham.

Starting with the Paris stories in which the repressed Caribbean experience came out unexpectedly or by indirection, we can see a more and more forthright admission and finally an avowal of the Caribbean material. This pattern is apparent in Rhys' arrangement of the stories in her collection *Sleep It Off Lady*, and in the choice of 'I Used to Live Here Once' as the closing piece. In this story, the woman who has returned to her island feels extraordinarily happy at the resumption of an intimate relationship:

> She was standing by the river looking at the stepping stones and remembering each one. There was the round unsteady stone, the pointed one, the flat one in the middle — the safe stone where you could stand and look round. The next wasn't so safe for when it showed dry it was slippery. But after that it was easy and soon she was standing on the other side.

The refusal of a boy and girl to acknowledge her, however, forces her to accept another part of the truth. She belongs to the place, and it belongs to her, but she has no more any special link with the people: 'Her arms went out instinctively with the longing to touch them ... Her arms fell to her sides as she watched them running across to the house. That was the first time she knew.' The title of the story can mean several things: I used to live here once, but that's over now; or I used to live here once, when I was here and when I'm not here ...' or I used to live here once and nobody can take this place from me'.

The stoic realisation that she belongs and does not belong, the reclaiming of an identity while accepting change and death, would seem to correspond with Jean Rhys' own discovery of her place at last.

The writing itself, started, stopped, and then resumed strongly, was an act of striving towards expansion, an assertion of innate healthy-mindedness expressing itself 'in the pleasure of unfolding one's capacities into the world, in the incorporation of things in the world, and in feeding on its limitless experiences'. Rhys' narrating techniques seem to have been chosen without theorising, though the evidence of the novel *Wide Sargasso Sea* indicates that she knew what she was about. The brilliant example of 'I Spy A Stranger' shows her capacity to invent the appropriate narrative method, and the careful unwinding and binding of 'Temps Perdi' exhibits a power to experiment with structure which she did not often feel the need to employ. But she fussed endlessly over the smaller items in her craft. Rhys' preoccupation with writing, finding the right word as she sometimes put it, is in evidence in a number of stories including 'The Lotus', 'On Not Shooting Sitting Birds', 'The Sound of the River', 'Tigers are Better Looking' and 'Let Them Call it Jazz'. In 'Tigers are Better Looking', Mr Severn has a false success at last as phrases suave and slick take the place of thoughts the journalist cannot bear to entertain, but the perfection of the story 'Let Them Call it Jazz', and the triumph of Selina Davis in the integrity of her song as an analogue for writing success, bring Rhys' concern with getting it right to a symbolic climax.

In making her peace with the region of her birth by a healing re-immersion in a sustaining landscape, Rhys finally belonged. In working at her craft to the end, she earned the death she wrote about earning in *Smile Please*: 'I must write. If I stop writing my life will have been an abject failure. It is that already to other people. But it could be an abject failure to myself. I will not have earned death.'

The stories have been arranged into groups and these put in a sequence not unlike that in Rhys' last collection *Sleep It Off Lady*.

The first item 'Invitation to the Dance' refers to a childhood game of love and chance which was banned by parents on moral grounds following a report made by a suspicious adult. More autobiography than fiction, 'Invitation to the Dance' serves as a prelude not least because, in addition to its content and form, it ends with a speculation on cultural influences and cultural mutation in the Caribbean.

Six stories make up the second group. All have a Caribbean setting – socio-historical and physical – and, in all, childhood experiences are prominent.

The third group contains three stories that may be called exile stories; their setting is England, but they all contain memories of, flashbacks to, or explicit statements about, the Caribbean. The earliest of these (not necessarily in order of composition) is 'Overture' which describes a fictional character's experiences at the Perse School, her arrival in England with an English aunt, an account of the decision that she should go to England, the death of her father, and her first job with a minor theatrical company. The second and third stories in the group fictionalize Jean Rhys' experiences more than the first, but all three stories relate in obvious ways to Rhys' own English experiences. In 'The Insect World', Rhys' life-long fear of tropical insects is fed into the jaundiced account by the author of a book *Nothing So Blue* which is being read by one of the characters; but, more significantly, we see the remembered insects and their activities being turned into an image of English people and their life styles.

In the fourth group there are four more exile stories. In this group, the fact that the protagonist comes from the Caribbean is not given prominence. In 'A Night', the suicidal heroine ('Make a hole in the water?') who feels out of place in Paris and in the world ('I don't belong here. I don't belong here. I must get out – must get out.') remembers in this hour of her need 'Saying the Litany to the Blessed Virgin which I learnt at the Convent and have never forgotten'. The main character in 'La Grosse Fifi' ('this girl was a funny one') speaks of English people as if she is not one, has the same name, Roseau, as the capital of Dominica and glosses it for her half-hearted companion: '"Yes, it suits me – it means a reed…A reed shaken by the wind. That's my motto, that is – are you going?"' Anna, the protagonist in 'Mannequin' is clearly a continuation from

Anna Morgan of the novel *Voyage in the Dark*. In the short story she listens ironically to the other mannequins talking about London and Londoners (she is the only one who doesn't speak during this conversation), and at the end of the story and at the end of the working day, as she steps out onto the Paris pavement 'the feeling that now she really belonged to the great, maddening city possessed her', a moment of happiness in which she joins the other mannequins in tropic blossoming 'pausing on the pavements a moment, making them as gay and beautiful as beds of flowers before they walked away and the Paris night swallowed them up'. There are better clues about the protagonist in 'Till September Petronella'. She admires the French girl Estelle who 'walked the tightrope so beautifully, not even knowing she was walking it,' a description which takes us back to Nina Rodriguez, a circus girl Jean Rhys had seen in Dominica during childhood and whom Rhys came to invest with symbolic and almost magical qualities. In 'Temps Perdi' Nina is advertised by the circus as 'the Only Girl Who Works Without a Net' and described in the author's voice as 'a black and gold butterfly caught in a web, weaving in and out of the web, miraculously escaping, miraculously coming to earth again.'

With 'Trio', 'Again the Antilles' and 'The Bishop's Feast' we see a return to the Caribbean setting.

In the final group I have placed for emphasis the long reflective encircling 'Temps Perdi', the stoic acceptance and implicit rootedness of 'I Used to Live Here Once' and the distillations in the created and detached work of art, 'Let Them Call it Jazz'.

Kenneth Ramchand

Invitation to the Dance

There weren't very many white families in Roseau but nearly all had their fair share of children, some as many as twelve. So, every fine afternoon a certain number of little girls and boys would be taken to the Botanical Gardens to play. I was one of them but, unlike the others, I was alone. Both my brothers and my elder sister had left the island. My younger sister was still a baby.

The nurses would sit on a bench and chatter. We would play, at first nearby, gradually getting farther and farther away until we were out of sight. The game I liked best was Looby Looby Li. I thought it better than Tug of War or any of the 'I-pick-you, I-pick-you' games which always ended in a quarrel, much more exciting than Kiss once, kiss twice, all fall down, which grew monotonous and didn't seem to lead anywhere.

Looby Li was a very energetic game, not to be played on hot afternoons. First, joining hands, we danced round in a ring, singing:

Will you dance Looby Looby Li
Will you dance Looby Looby Li
Will you dance Looby Looby Li
As you did last night?

Then we sang the verses. For Looby Li was about the game of love and chance. Each verse described some variation of the game and after each we'd try to act out the enigmatic, scarcely understood words we'd sung. Then we'd join hands again for the chorus: 'Will you dance Looby Looby Li, etc....As you did last night?'

I for one pranced about in all innocence. So, I think, did most of the others, and I was very surprised when one day my mother asked me: 'Do you ever play a game called Looby Li?' I said yes, we did, and that it was a good game and that I liked it.

She asked: 'Who started it? Who taught you the words?' I answered truthfully that I didn't remember, I didn't know; but immediately added: 'Perhaps it was Willie.'

She said: 'Willie? Well, I'm surprised at Willie, I'm astonished at Willie. Where did he pick it up?' But I was miserably wondering why I had told such a lie. For it wasn't Willie and I liked him the best. I didn't want to get him into any sort of trouble. Why had I said it was Willie when it wasn't Willie? I don't remember the rest of the conversation but it ended by her saying that whoever had started it, I must never play it again. Never. It was the reverse of a good game. It was a wicked game and I must forget all about it. 'Now promise me,' she said, then went off forgetting apparently that I hadn't promised anything at all.

Very soon after this, it may have been the next day, when afternoon came at the Botanical Gardens, some suggested playing Looby Looby Li. But the older girls and boys gathered in a group whispering and giggling. Finally one of them announced that he was sick of Looby Li, that it was a silly game, a baby's game, a lot of rubbish. 'Let's play something else. Let's play Tug of War.' But in spite of all this camouflage, everyone soon knew what had happened. Some man or some woman – impossible to know – had watched us playing, then gone away to report that we played disgusting games, sang disgusting songs, that the nurses were lazy brutes, sprawled on the benches gossiping, and didn't care what we did or even know where we went. Most of the children had been spoken to and the older ones decided that Looby Li wasn't worth the trouble and we wouldn't play it any more.

But even when I grew older I remembered and thought about it. Was it a negro song? Was it a negro version of a French song? I didn't think so. At the time I'm writing of, West Indian music had far more of a Spanish rhythm than it has now. But Spanish, American, or African, it was always sad. Looby Li was a quick dancing tune, full of gaiety and light-heartedness. I know it wasn't any sort of a negro sound. Later, when I was fascinated by novels of the Middle Ages, I decided that it was an English song of very long ago, before Cromwell and the Puritans, before Henry VIII and the Reformation. Sung in the remote country, it had trickled down the centuries, trickled out to the West Indies, there at last to die, or to be changed out of all knowledge like so many other things. Try as I may I can't remember who taught us the words and the music or why I said 'Willie' when it wasn't Willie.

Mixing Cocktails

The house in the hills was very new and very ugly, long and narrow, of unpainted wood, perched oddly on high posts, I think as a protection from wood ants. There were six rooms with a verandah that ran the whole length of the house.... But when you went up there, there was always the same sensation of relief and coolness – in the ugly house with the beginnings of a rose garden, after an hour's journey by boat and another hour and a half on horse-back, climbing slowly up....

On the verandah, upon a wooden table with four stout legs, stood an enormous brass telescope. With it you spied out the steamers passing: the French mail on its way to Guadeloupe, the Canadian, the Royal Mail, which should have been stately and was actually the shabbiest of the lot.... Or an exciting stranger!

At night one gazed through it at the stars and pretended to be interested.... 'That's Venus.... Oh, is that Venus.... And that's the Southern Cross....' An unloaded shotgun leant up in one corner; there were always plenty of straw rockingchairs and a canvas hammock with many cushions.

From the verandah one looked down the green valley sloping to the sea, but from the other side of the house one could only see the mountains, lovely but melancholy as mountains always are to a child.

Lying in the hammock, swinging cautiously for the ropes creaked, one dreamt.... The morning dream was the best – very early, before the sun was properly up. The sea was then a very tender blue, like the dress of the Virgin Mary, and on it were little white triangles. The fishing boats.

A very short dream, the morning dream – mostly about what one would do with the endless blue day. One would

bathe in the pool: perhaps one would find treasure....
Morgan's Treasure. For who does not know that, just before
he was captured and I think hung at Kingston, Jamaica,
Morgan buried his treasure in the Dominican mountains.... A
wild place, Dominica. Savage and lost. Just the place for
Morgan to hide his treasure in.

It was very difficult to look at the sea in the middle of the
day. The light made it so flash and glitter: it was necessary to
screw the eyes up tight before looking. Everything was still
and languid, worshipping the sun.

The midday dream was languid too – vague, tinged with
melancholy as one stared at the hard, blue, blue sky. It was
sure to be interrupted by someone calling to one to come in out
of the sun. One was not to sit in the sun. One had been told not
to be in the sun.... One would one day regret freckles.

So the late afternoon was the best time on the verandah, but
it was spoiled for all the rest were there....

So soon does one learn the bitter lesson that humanity is
never content just to differ from you and let it go at that.
Never. They must interfere, actively and grimly, between your
thoughts and yourself – with the passionate wish to level up
everything and everybody.

I am speaking to you; do you not hear? You must break
yourself of your habit of never listening. You have such an
absent-minded expression. Try not to look vague....

So rude!

The English aunt gazes and exclaims at intervals: 'The
colours.... How exquisite!... Extraordinary that so few people
should visit the West Indies.... That *sea*.... Could anything be
more lovely?'

It is a purple sea with a sky to match it. The Caribbean. The
deepest, the loveliest in the world....

Sleepily but tactfully, for she knows it delights my father,
she admires the roses, the hibiscus, the humming birds. Then
she starts to nod. She is always falling asleep, at the oddest
moments. It is the unaccustomed heat.

I should like to laugh at her, but I am a well-behaved little
girl.... Too well-behaved.... I long to be like Other People! The
extraordinary, ungetatable, oddly cruel Other People, with
their way of wantonly hurting and then accusing you of being

thin-skinned, sulky, vindictive or ridiculous. All because a hurt and puzzled little girl has retired into her shell.

The afternoon dream is a materialistic óne…. It is of the days when one shall be plump and beautiful instead of pale and thin: perfectly behaved instead of awkward…. When one will wear sweeping dresses and feathered hats and put gloves on with ease and delight…. And of course, of one's marriage: the dark moustache and perfectly creased trousers…. Vague, that.

The verandah gets dark very quickly. The sun sets: at once night and the fireflies.

A warm, velvety, sweet-smelling night, but frightening and disturbing if one is alone in the hammock. Ann Twist, our cook, the old obeah woman, has told me: 'You all must'n look too much at de moon….'

If you fall asleep in the moonlight you are bewitched, it seems…the moon does bad things to you if it shines on you when you sleep. Repeated often….

So, shivering a little, I go into the room for the comfort of my father working out his chess problem from *The Times Weekly Edition*. Then comes my nightly duty of mixing cocktails.

In spite of my absentmindedness I mix cocktails very well and swizzle them better (our cocktails, in the West Indies, are drunk frothing, and the instrument with which one froths them is called a swizzle-stick) than anyone else in the house.

I measure out angostura and gin, feeling important and happy, with an uncanny intuition as to how strong I must make each separate drink.

Here then is something I can do…. Action, they say, is more worthy than dreaming….

Fishy Waters

THE EDITOR
The Dominica Herald

March 3rd, 189—

Dear Sir,

Yesterday I heard a piece of news that appalled me. It seems that a British workman, Mr Longa by name, who arrived a year ago, has been arrested and is being held by the police. Mr Longa is a carpenter. He is also a socialist, and does not disguise his political opinions. It goes without saying that a certain class of person in this island, who seem to imagine that the colour of their skins enables them to behave like gods, disliked and disapproved of him from the first. He was turned out of Miss Lambton's boarding-house after one night and had the greatest difficulty in finding anywhere to live. Eventually he settled in a predominantly negro quarter – another cause for offence. A determined effort was made to induce him to leave the island. When this failed, with their usual hypocrisy they pretended to ignore him, but they were merely biding their time.

He was found joking roughly with one of the many vagabond children who infest the streets of Roseau, and is to be accused of child-molesting and cruelty, if you please. A trumped-up charge, on the face of it. In this way, they plan to be rid of a long-standing nuisance and to be able to boast about their even-handed justice. The hypocrisy of these people, who bitterly resent that they no longer have the power over the bodies and minds of the blacks they once had (the cruelty of West Indian planters was a by-word), making a scape-goat of an honest British workman, is enough to make any decent person's gorge rise. A London barrister, new to this island, has offered to defend Mr Longa without charge. Only one just man among so many?

Yours truly,
Disgusted

THE EDITOR
The Dominica Herald   March 10, 189—

Dear Sir,
   Who is 'Disgusted'? Who is this person (I believe people) who tries to stir up racial hatred whenever possible? Almost invariably with gloating satisfaction, they will drag in the horrors of the slave trade. Who would think, to hear them talk, that slavery was abolished by the English nearly a hundred years ago? They are long on diatribes, but short on facts. The slave trade was an abominable one, but it could not have existed without the help and cooperation of African chiefs. Slavery still exists, and is taken for granted, in Africa, both among negroes and Arabs. Are these facts ever mentioned? The bad is endlessly repeated and insisted upon; the good is ridiculed, forgotten or denied. Who does this, and why?

Yours truly,
Ian J. MacDonald

THE EDITOR
The Dominica Herald   March 17th, 189—

Dear Sir,
   It is sometimes said that African chiefs probably had a good deal to do with the slave trade, but I have never heard before that this was proven. In his typical letter I notice that Mr MacDonald places all the blame on these perhaps mythical Africans and says nothing about the greed of white merchants or the abominable cruelty and indifference of white planters. The treatment meted out to Mr Longa shows that their heirs and successors have not changed all that much.

Yours truly,
P. Kelly
Kelly's Universal Stores

THE EDITOR
The Dominica Herald   March 24th, 189—

Dear Sir,

I hate to interfere with the amusement of your readers, but I must point out that according to English law it is highly improper to discuss a case that has not been tried (*sub judice*). In this country the custom seems to be more honoured in the breach than in the observance.

Yours truly,
Fiat Justicia

This correspondence is now closed. *Editor*.

On the same day the editor, who was known as Papa Dom, remarked in a leading article: 'These are fishy waters – very fishy waters.'

6 Cork Street
Roseau, Dominica   March 24th, 189—

My dear Caroline,

Your letter rescued me from a mood of great depression. I am answering it at once – it will be such a relief to tell you about something that I don't care to discuss with people here.

You wouldn't remember a man called Jimmy Longa – he arrived soon after you left. Well, Matt found him trying to saw a little girl in two – can you believe it? – and is to be the main witness for the prosecution. The whole place is buzzing with gossip, arguments, letters to the local newspaper and so on. It is most unpleasant. I've begged Matt to have nothing further to do with it, I'm sure there'll be trouble. He says why should there be, Longa's a white man not a black one. I say 'Jimmy Longa will be an honorary black before this is over, you'll see. They'll twist it somehow.' But he won't even talk about it now. I'm not at all happy about Matt. He doesn't look well and is so unlike what he used to be. I begin to wish I'd never persuaded him to settle here when he retired – a visit to escape the winter is one thing, living here is quite another.

The first scandal about Longa was that Miss Lambton turned him out as he got so drunk every night. He's a jobbing carpenter, quite a good one when he's sober, so he soon found a place to live and got plenty of work. His story is that he's on his way to America and stopped off at Dominica to make some money. I wonder who on earth could have advised him to do that! He gave out that he was a socialist, extreme – the new world must be built on the ashes of the old, that sort of thing. He preached fire and slaughter in the rum-shop and everywhere else so you can imagine he wasn't very popular with the white people. Then he got malaria badly and Miss Lambton, who had him on her conscience, went to the hospital to see how he was. She said he looked very ill and told her that his only wish now was to get back to England, but he couldn't raise the money. She started a subscription for him and headed the list with £10, which she certainly couldn't afford. Nearly everyone chipped in and a good deal was raised. But somehow he managed to persuade Miss Lambton to hand the lot over directly. Then disappeared. There was no case against him – he'd been careful not to promise or sign anything – besides, a lot of people thought it comic. They said 'Poor Mamie Lambton, it seems she's very upset. But what a chap! You have to laugh!' Even when he reappeared, more fanatical than ever, nobody took him seriously – he was the Dominica funny story. And now this.

I've got one piece of pleasant news. Because Matt dislikes the town so much we've bought a small estate in the country where he may be happier. It's called Three Rivers – an old place, and as usual the house is falling to bits. It's being fixed up – but lately I've wondered if we'll ever live there.

No one at home would understand why all this is looming over me so much, but you know the kind of atmosphere we get here sometimes, so I think you will.

I'm so glad you are happy and don't feel the cold too much. Perhaps the next time I write it will all be over and I'll be more cheerful.

Meanwhile I send you my love,
Affectionately,
Maggie

The day after Jimmy Longa's trial there was a long report on the front page of the *Dominica Herald*. The reporter, having remarked on the crowded court-room, usually empty for assault and battery cases, went on to say that the prosecuting counsel, M. Didier of Roseau, had seemed so nervous at first that he was almost inaudible. His speech was short. He said that it was fortunate that there had been an eye-witness to the attack on the child, Josephine Mary Dent, known as Jojo, for though Mr Longa's activities were common knowledge in Roseau, no one had dared to come forward to accuse him, a white man. 'There are a certain number of children, abandoned and unprotected, roaming the streets. This child was one of them. The accused is a danger to all children, but these are particularly at risk.' M. Didier asked for a sentence heavy enough to deter possible imitators. He then called his first witness, Mr Matthew Penrice.

Mr Penrice said that on the late afternoon of February 27th he was walking up Jetty Street on the way to the Club when he heard a child screaming in a very distressing way. As he approached the house the screams came from, the sound stopped abruptly – no angry voices, complete silence. The house stood well back from the empty street, and there was a fence round it. It occurred to him that a child, left alone there, might have met with an accident, and on an impulse he knocked at the wooden gate. There was no answer so he pushed the gate open. As he did so he heard a man say: 'Now I'm going to saw you in two, like they do in English music halls.' The yard of the house was quite a large one; there was a tree in the corner, and under the tree a plank raised up on trestles. A naked little negro girl lay on the plank, her head hanging over the end. She was silent, and her face was almost green with fright. The man's back was to him and the saw in his hand was touching the child's waist. Mr Penrice called out 'What the devil's going on here?' The man turned, dropping the saw, and he recognized Mr Longa, who was not in court. Mr Longa said: 'I wasn't going to hurt her – I was only joking.' He had been holding the child on the plank, and when he turned she rolled off and lay on the ground without moving. Mr Longa repeated that it was a joke. When the witness approached the unconscious child he saw that her body was covered with bruises. He did not speak to Mr Longa again, but wrapped the child in his jacket and took her to the house of Madame Octavia Joseph, which was close by. He then sent for the doctor who fortunately was able to come at once. After the doctor had arrived he went to the police station and reported what he had seen.

Cross-examined by counsel for the defence, Mr Penrice was asked if Jetty Street was his usual way to the Club. He answered that it was not, but he was in a hurry to keep an appointment and Jetty Street was a short cut.

Counsel asked him: 'Would it surprise you to know that information from your household reveals that on that particular day you left for the Club very much earlier than usual? The domestic remembers it clearly, as it was her birthday. As your habits are so regular, she wondered why you had left the house on foot on such a hot day, nearly two hours earlier than usual. Why, then, did you have to take a short cut?'

Mr Penrice replied: 'Two hours is an exaggeration. I left my house earlier than usual to go for a walk – I don't mind the heat – and I forgot the time, so I was trying to get to the Club as quickly as I could.'

'When you heard the accused say "Like they do in English music halls", was he aware that anyone was listening?'

'No, he didn't know that I was there.'

'So he was speaking to the child?'

'I suppose so.'

'Do you know that there is a popular trick on the English music halls when a girl is supposed to be sawn in two?'

'Yes, I think so.'

'And is anyone ever sawn in two, or hurt in any way?'

'Of course not. It's a trick.'

'Perhaps you were too startled and shocked to realize that when the accused said "As they do in English music halls" he was really declaring that what he was about to do was not to be taken seriously. It was a joke.'

'It was not a joke.'

'And why are you so sure of that?'

'When the man faced me, I knew that it was not a joke at all.'

'I see. But is there not a certain amount of prejudice against Mr Longa in this island? Are you not very ready to believe the worst of him? Has there not been a great deal of gossip about him?'

'I only know Mr Longa by sight. The gossip here does not interest me.'

'So you are not – shall we say – prejudiced?'

'No, not at all. Not in the way you mean.'

'I am glad to hear it. Now, as you say the child was unconscious and badly hurt, would not the normal thing have been either to take or to send her to the hospital?'

'I didn't think of the hospital. Madame Joseph's house was nearby and I knew she would be well looked-after so I took her there and sent for the doctor.'

'Mr Penrice, has Madame Joseph ever been in your service?'

'Yes. She was with us for nearly five years, off and on, when we used to winter here before making it our home. That was why I was so sure that she was not only a kind woman, but a perfectly reliable one.'

'When she left your employment, did you give her a large present of money?'

'Not large, no. Both my wife and myself thought she had given us invaluable service. She was no longer in very good health, so we were happy to give her enough to buy a small house, where she would be comfortable and secure.'

'No doubt she was very grateful?'

'I think she was pleased, yes.'

'As she was so indebted to you, you must have been sure that in an emergency any instructions you gave her would be carried out?'

'In saying that, you only show that you know nothing at all about the people of this island. Madame Joseph is a most independent woman. Even if I – or rather, we – had installed her in a palace instead of a small house, she would not have thought herself bound to follow my instructions. No.'

'And it really seemed to you proper to leave a badly injured child in the care of an ex-servant, however devoted, who had no medical knowledge and no experience of nursing?'

'I did what I thought best for her.'

'And did you tell the doctor that you had taken her there because Madame Joseph was the child's close relative?'

'I did nothing of the sort.'

'But you can imply a thing without actually saying it, can you not?'

'You most certainly can.'

'Thank you, Mr Penrice. You may stand down.'

Mr Penrice was followed in the witness box by Madame Octavia Joseph, a dignified woman who gave her evidence clearly and obviously made a favourable impression on the magistrate, Mr Somers. When she saw the state the little girl was in, she said, she understood why Mr Penrice was going to the police. 'It was a very wicked person did that.' Soon after the doctor came the child recovered consciousness, but at once began to tremble and scream. Having treated her bruises, the doctor gave her a sedative, said he would call next day, that she was to see nobody, and that she was not to be questioned until she was better. Madame Joseph had done her best to follow the doctor's orders and had taken great care of the child, whose condition was much improved; 'But she says she does not remember anything about being attacked. When I told her she ought to try to remember, she only began to cry and shake, so I thought it better for the doctor to speak to her.'

The last witness for the prosecution, Dr Trevor, said that on the evening of February 27th he had been at home when he got a message to come at once to 11 Hill Street to treat a badly injured child. When he first saw the child she had fainted and obviously been savagely beaten. When she recovered consciousness she was so frightened and hysterical that after treating her he gave her a sedative. She was probably about eleven or twelve years of age, but as she was very thin and undernourished, she may have been a year or two older.

Counsel asked Dr Trevor: 'Have you seen the child since?'

'Yes, on several occasions.'

'When did you see her last?'

'I saw her yesterday.'

'And what did you think of her?'

'I found that her condition had greatly improved. She has

been carefully looked after and is well on the way to recovery. Already she seems quite a different child.'

'When you visited this child, did you ever question her or ask her who had attacked her?'

'Yes, after I thought she was better I did question her, of course. She always behaved in the same way. She says she has forgotten. I tried two or three times to question her more closely – the only result is that she becomes frightened, hysterical and quite incoherent.'

'When you questioned the child, was Madam Joseph with you?'

'She was there the first time, but I have often been alone with the child and this is invariably the way she behaves.'

'Did it strike you at all that because of what has happened, she had been mentally affected?'

'No, I saw no signs of that. She'd probably be quite a bright little thing, given a chance.'

'Did you not think it somewhat strange that although she is so much better, she still refuses to say anything about what happened to her?'

'Perhaps it is not as strange as you think. Some people after a great shock or fright will talk volubly, others "clam up" as they say in parts of England. She'll probably talk eventually, but it's impossible to say when.'

'And you find nothing unusual about this "clamming up", as you call it?'

'I have known cases when, after a frightening and harmful experience, the mind has protected itself by forgetting. If you try to force recollection, the patient becomes agitated and resentful.'

'Do you really think that this interesting, but rather complicated theory could apply to a negro child, completely illiterate, only eleven or twelve years of age? Is it not more likely that she remains silent because she has either been persuaded or threatened – probably a bit of both – not to talk?'

'I do not believe that the result of illiteracy is an uncomplicated mind – far from it. And I do not know who you are suggesting could have frightened her. My orders were that she should be kept perfectly quiet and see no one except Madame Joseph, whose house is surrounded by inquisitive neighbours. If anyone else had been there I would have been told, believe me. The child certainly isn't at all afraid of Madame Joseph. On the contrary, she seems to trust her, even be attached to her – insofar as a child like that can trust or be attached at all. However, if you are not satisfied with my evidence, why not question the child? In my opinion you will get nothing at all out of her and may do her harm, but you must decide for yourself.'

Here Mr Somers intervened and said that the child must certainly not be questioned by anyone as long as the doctor thought it might be harmful.

Counsel then asked Dr Trevor: 'Were you led to believe that the child had been taken to Madame Joseph's house because she was a close relative?'

'No. I suppose I took it for granted. In any case, I made no suggestion that she should be moved. I thought she was in very good hands.'

Counsel for the Defence, Mr Berkeley, said that his client was too ill to appear in Court, but that he would read his statement. This, he submitted, was a complete answer to the charge.

Mr Longa's Statement: 'I had not felt very well that day. It was too hot, so I thought I'd knock off for a bit. But as I might be able to work later on when it was cooler, I left my saw in the yard, with a plank I was working on to make bookshelves. I was very thirsty and had a few drinks, then I fell asleep. I don't know how long I slept before loud screams woke me up, coming from my yard. The noise these children make is very trying and that's putting it mildly. They climb over the fence into the yard to play, and get up to all kinds of mischief. I'd chase them away, but they always came back. They'd follow me in the street, jeering and laughing, and several times I've been stoned. I don't deny I've grown to dislike them very much indeed.

'I got up feeling shaky and in a bad temper, and in my yard I found a little girl lying on the ground, screaming. I asked her what was the matter several times, but she took no notice at all and went on yelling. At last I told her to shut up, get out, and go and scream somewhere else. She wouldn't even look at me, and the noise she was making went through and through my head, so I lost my temper, picked her up and put her on the plank, telling her I was going to saw her in two, but I didn't really mean to hurt her and I told her so. I didn't notice anything wrong with her, or think it strange that she was naked – they very often are, especially on hot days. No, I never meant to hurt her. But I hoped to frighten her a bit, and that she'd tell the others, and then perhaps they'd leave me in peace. These children had made my life a misery, and I wanted to stop them from doing it. I swear that was all I meant – to frighten her. It was just a joke. When Mr Penrice came and accused me I was too confused to say much. I told him I hadn't meant any harm but he wouldn't listen to me, nor would the policemen when they arrested me. I am sorry for what I did and for frightening her, but I had been drinking. I quite lost my temper and was very angry. That is what happened, and that is the truth.'

To this Mr Berkeley added that Mr Longa was now very willing to leave the island. 'He says that even in England he would not be treated with such injustice. As to the rumours about my client, I am surprised that my learned friend has mentioned them, as he has failed to produce a single witness to substantiate them. Without wishing to impugn Mr Penrice's word, I must point out that there is no evidence at all that Mr Longa was the child's attacker. She may have run into the empty yard to hide, or – more likely – she was thrown there by a real attacker who then made off, feeling certain that Mr Longa would be accused. Mr Penrice admits that he heard Mr Longa saying "As they do in English music halls" before he knew anyone was listening. This seems to me to prove conclusively that Mr Longa's behaviour was a joke – a rough, even a cruel joke if you like, but certainly not deserving of several years imprisonment in a gaol not fit for any human being, Englishman or not.'

Mr Berkeley ended by saying that Mr Longa was a very intelligent man left terribly alone and isolated – also he was not a well man. It was hardly surprising that he turned to rum for consolation, and easy to believe that, woken suddenly, he felt extremely irritable and behaved in a way that was not normal to him.

The Summing-up. The magistrate, Mr Somers, said that this was
a very disturbing case. 'There is no direct evidence that it was
Mr Longa who first attacked the child, causing the extensive
bruising. He denies it strongly, and the child cannot yet be
questioned. I find his statement as read by Counsel for the
Defence convincing up to a point. Two things, however, strike
me as unlikely. Why should he think that this unfortunate
child would know anything about English music halls or the
tricks performed there? Why should his mentioning them
reassure her? It probably added to her fright. Also, and more
important: However drunk he was, could he have picked up a
badly injured naked child and carried her to the plank without
noticing the marks on her body? According to Mr Longa he
noticed nothing, but proceeded with his savage joke. I find
this so unlikely as to be almost incredible. He excuses himself
by saying that he had been drinking, but he is a man
accustomed to strong drink and there is no report of advanced
intoxication from the police who arrested him.

'I am not here to speculate and I cannot accept either hearsay
evidence or innuendoes supported by no evidence; but I have
not been in my post for twenty years without learning that it is
extremely difficult to obtain direct evidence here. Often a
criminal is quite well-known but the police find it impossible to
produce a single witness against him. There is, unfortunately,
in these islands a great distrust both of the police and of the
law.'

Here a voice interrupted: 'Can you blame them?' and there
was hubbub in the Court. Several women were in tears. Order
was only restored when a threat was made to clear the Court.

Mr Somers continued: 'We can only hope that this perhaps
natural distrust will diminish with time. In view of my doubts I
am glad to hear that Mr Longa is willing to leave the island. I
direct that his passage to Southampton be paid by the
Government. Until he sails he must remain in custody of the
police, but must be allowed to receive visitors. He must be able
to get food or provisions from outside and care must be taken
to restore him to health. I am sure that his able Counsel will see
that my instructions are carried out.'

The crowd was subdued and less talkative than usual as it
left the court-room, but a group of rowdies shouted at Mr

Penrice as he came out. He took no notice of this demonstration, but got into his waiting trap and drove off. A few stones were thrown after him, but the rowdies quickly dispersed when a policeman intervened.

'I bet you anything Mamie Lambton's going to start another subscription,' said Matthew Penrice to his wife when he got home. He added: 'Don't look so gloomy, Maggie. I've one piece of very good news. Octavia tells me that she's been corresponding with an old friend in St Lucia with no children of her own who wishes to adopt Jojo. She's quite sure of this woman and says it'll be the best thing possible. I think so too. She's get right away from all the gossip and questioning here, and start again. I'll see to it that she gets there as soon as she's well enough. I'll take care of everything, don't worry.'

Maggie Penrice watched the negro maid Janet pile the coffee things onto the tray and walk out, silent, bare-footed. When she had said 'What delicious coffee, Janet,' the girl hadn't answered, hadn't even smiled. But they don't smile here, they laugh, they seldom smile. Not smilers with a knife. No? Even when they were alone she didn't speak, but went on folding and unfolding the letter. She re-read the last paragraph.

'Thank you for the money you sent. I will keep it faithfully and carefully for her when she grows up and thank you from my heart for giving her to me. You would be pleased to see her. She is getting quite fat and pretty and hardly ever wakes up screaming as she used to do. I now close and say no more from my over-flowing heart. Wishing you and your amiable lady all health and prosperity. Anine Dib.'

Maggie said: 'Dib. What a funny name.'

'Syrian, probably,' Matt said. 'Well, that's the last of that, I hope, and now you mustn't worry any more. Much the best thing that could have happened. Surely you agree?'

'Perhaps…. But Matt, do you think it was wise to send her away quite so quickly?'

'The sooner the better, I should have thought. Why not?'

The room was at the back of the house, there was no noise from the street. It was hot and airless and the blinds were half drawn. She folded the letter carefully and put it back into its envelope, then pushed it across to him.

'Because it's all over the place that Octavia's in your pay and that you both sent the child to St Lucia so that there was no chance of her ever talking. They're saying that you did it and pushed it off onto Jimmy Longa. The whole thing is utterly ridiculous, of course, but you ought to stop it.'

'Stop it? What do you want me to do? How can I stop it?'

'Surely that wouldn't be too hard. It's so absurd. How could you have done it – how is it even possible?'

'Do you think these damnable hogs care whether it's possible or not, or how or where or when? They've just got hold of something to grunt about, that's all. If you think I'm going to argue with this lot you must be mad. I've had more than enough of this whole damned place. If you really want to know what I feel, I want to clear out. It's not this particular storm in a tea-cup that's decided me. I've wanted to leave for some time, and you must have known.'

'They'll say you've run away.'

'God, can't you get it into your head that I don't give a damn what they say here? Oh come on, Maggie, don't look like that. I know how you feel, how you dread the cold, how much better you are here, and its beauty and all that – I only wish I felt like you, but to me it's suffocating.'

'Yes, I know. But I hoped you'd feel better when we left Roseau.'

'The hatred would be exactly the same in the country – suppressed, perhaps. If you don't want to leave you needn't. I won't sell Three Rivers or this house, and the money will be all right – surely you know that?'

'But Matt, you find envy, malice, hatred everywhere. You can't escape.'

'Perhaps, but I'm sick of this particular brand.'

'Do you think I'd want to stay here by myself if you went? Do you really think that?'

He didn't answer but smiled and said: 'Then that's settled.' He patted her shoulder lightly, then he went over to an armchair, took up a book; but Maggie, watching him anxiously, cautiously, saw that he never turned a page. Suddenly she screwed up her eyes tightly and shook her head. She was trying to fight the overwhelming certainty that the man she was looking at was a complete stranger.

Heat

Ash had fallen. Perhaps it had fallen the night before or perhaps it was still falling. I can only remember in patches. I was looking at it two feet deep on the flat roof outside my bedroom. The ash and the silence. Nobody talked in the street, nobody talked while we ate, or hardly at all. I know now that they were all frightened. They thought our volcano was going up.

Our volcano was called the boiling lake. That's what it was, a sheet of water that always boiled. From what fires? I thought of it as a mysterious place that few people had ever seen. In the churchyard where we often went – for death was not then a taboo subject – quite near the grave of my little sister, was a large marble headstone. 'Sacred to the memory of Clive —, who lost his life at the boiling lake in Dominica in an heroic attempt to save his guide'. Aged twenty-seven. I remember that too.

He was a young Englishman, a visitor, who had gone exploring with two guides to the boiling lake. As they were standing looking at it one of the guides, who was a long way ahead, staggered and fell. The other seized hold of the Englishman's hand and said 'Run!' There must have been some local tradition that poisonous gases sometimes came out of the lake. After a few steps the Englishman pulled his hand away and went back and lifted up the man who had fallen. Then he too staggered and they both fell. The surviving guide ran and told what had happened.

In the afternoon two little friends were coming to see us and to my surprise they both arrived carrying large glass bottles. Both the bottles had carefully written labels pasted on: 'Ash collected from the streets of Roseau on May 8th, 1902.' The

little boy asked me if I'd like to have his jar, but I refused. I
didn't want to touch the ash. I don't remember the rest of the
day. I must have gone to bed, for that night my mother woke
me and without saying anything, led me to the window. There
was a huge black cloud over Martinique. I couldn't ever
describe that cloud, so huge and black it was, but I have never
forgotten it. There was no moon, no stars, but the edges of the
cloud were flame-coloured and in the middle what looked to
me like lightning flickered, never stopping. My mother said:
'You will never see anything like this in your life again.' That
was all. I must have gone to sleep at the window and been
carried to bed.

Next morning we heard what had happened. Was it a blue
or a grey day? I only know ash wasn't falling any longer. The
Roseau fishermen went out very early, as they did in those
days. They met the fishermen from Port de France, who knew.
That was how we heard before the cablegrams, the papers and
all the rest came flooding in. That was how we heard of Mont
Pelée's eruption and the deaths of 40,000 people, and that
there was nothing left of St Pierre.

As soon as ships were sailing again between Dominica and
Martinique my father went to see the desolation that was left.
He brought back a pair of candlesticks, tall heavy brass
candlesticks which must have been in a church. The heat had
twisted them into an extraordinary shape. He hung them on
the wall of the dining-room and I stared at them all through
meals, trying to make sense of the shape.

It was after this that the gossip started. That went on for
years so I can remember it well. St Pierre, they said, was a very
wicked city. It had not only a theatre, but an opera house,
which was probably wickeder still. Companies from Paris
performed there. But worse than this was the behaviour of the
women who were the prettiest in the West Indies. They tied
their turbans in a particular way, a sort of language of love that
all St Pierre people understood. Tied in one way it meant 'I am
in love, I am not free'; tied in another way it meant 'You are
welcome, I am free'. Even the women who were married, or as
good as, tied their kerchiefs in the 'I am free' way. And that
wasn't all. The last bishop who had visited the city had taken
off his shoes and solemnly shaken them over it. After that, of

course, you couldn't wonder.

As I grew older I heard of a book by a man called Lafcadio Hearn who had written about St Pierre as it used to be, about Ti Marie and all the others, but I never found the book and stopped looking for it. However, one day I did discover a pile of old newspapers and magazines, some illustrated: the English version of the eruption. They said nothing about the opera house or the theatre which must have seemed to the English the height of frivolity in a Caribbean island, and very little about the city and its inhabitants. It was nearly all about the one man who had survived. He was a convict imprisoned in an underground cell, so he escaped – the only one out of 40,000. He was now travelling round the music-halls of the world being exhibited. They had taught him a little speech. He must be quite a rich man – what did he do with his money? Would he marry again? His wife and children had been killed in the eruption…. I read all this then I thought but it wasn't like that, it wasn't like that at all.

The Day They Burned the Books

My friend Eddie was a small, thin boy. You could see the blue veins in his wrists and temples. People said that he had consumption and wasn't long for this world. I loved, but sometimes despised him.

His father, Mr Sawyer, was a strange man. Nobody could make out what he was doing in our part of the world at all. He was not a planter or a doctor or a lawyer or a banker. He didn't keep a store. He wasn't a schoolmaster or a government official. He wasn't – that was the point – a gentleman. We had several resident romantics who had fallen in love with the moon on the Caribbees – they were all gentlemen and quite unlike Mr Sawyer who hadn't an 'h' in his composition. Besides, he detested the moon and everything else about the Caribbean and he didn't mind telling you so.

He was agent for a small steamship line which in those days linked up Venezuela and Trinidad with the smaller islands, but he couldn't make much out of that. He must have a private income, people decided, but they never decided why he had chosen to settle in a place he didn't like and to marry a coloured woman. Though a decent, respectable, nicely educated coloured woman, mind you.

Mrs Sawyer must have been very pretty once but, what with one thing and another, that was in days gone by.

When Mr Sawyer was drunk – this often happened – he used to be very rude to her. She never answered him.

'Look at the nigger showing off,' he would say; and she would smile as if she knew she ought to see the joke but couldn't. 'You damned, long-eyed gloomy half-caste, you don't smell right,' he would say; and she never answered, not even to whisper, 'You don't smell right to me, either.'

The story went that once they had ventured to give a dinner party and that when the servant, Mildred, was bringing in coffee, he had pulled Mrs Sawyer's hair. 'Not a wig, you see,' he bawled. Even then, if you can believe it, Mrs Sawyer had laughed and tried to pretend that it was all part of the joke, this mysterious, obscure, sacred English joke.

But Mildred told the other servants in the town that her eyes had gone wicked, like a soucriant's eyes, and that afterwards she had picked up some of the hair he pulled out and put it in an envelope, and that Mr Sawyer ought to look out (hair is obeah as well as hands).

Of course, Mrs Sawyer had her compensations. They lived in a very pleasant house in Hill Street. The garden was large and they had a fine mango tree, which bore prolifically. The fruit was small, round, very sweet and juicy – a lovely, red-and-yellow colour when it was ripe. Perhaps it was one of the compensations, I used to think.

Mr Sawyer built a room on to the back of this house. It was unpainted inside and the wood smelt very sweet. Bookshelves lined the walls. Every time the Royal Mail steamer came in it brought a package for him, and gradually the empty shelves filled.

Once I went there with Eddie to borrow *The Arabian Nights*. That was on a Saturday afternoon, one of those hot, still afternoons when you felt that everything had gone to sleep, even the water in the gutters. But Mrs Sawyer was not asleep. She put her head in at the door and looked at us, and I knew that she hated the room and hated the books.

It was Eddie with the pale blue eyes and straw-coloured hair – the living image of his father, though often as silent as his mother – who first infected me with doubts about 'home', meaning England. He would be so quiet when others who had never seen it – none of us had ever seen it – were talking about its delights, gesticulating freely as we talked – London, the beautiful, rosy-cheeked ladies, the theatres, the shops, the fog, the blazing coal fires in winter, the exotic food (whitebait eaten to the sound of violins), strawberries and cream – the word 'strawberries' always spoken with a guttural and throaty sound which we imagined to be the proper English pronunciation.

'I don't like strawberries,' Eddie said on one occasion.

'You *don't like* strawberries?'

'No, and I don't like daffodils either. Dad's always going on about them. He says they lick the flowers here into a cocked hat and I bet that's a lie.'

We were all too shocked to say, 'You don't know a thing about it.' We were so shocked that nobody spoke to him for the rest of the day. But I for one admired him. I also was tired of learning and reciting poems in praise of daffodils, and my relations with the few 'real' English boys and girls I had met were awkward. I had discovered that if I called myself English they would snub me haughtily: 'You're not English; you're a horrid colonial.' 'Well, I don't much want to be English,' I would say. 'It's much more fun to be French or Spanish or something like that – and, as a matter of fact, I am a bit.' Then I was too killingly funny, quite ridiculous. Not only a horrid colonial, but also ridiculous. Heads I win, tails you lose – that was the English. I had thought about all this, and thought hard, but I had never dared to tell anybody what I thought and I realized that Eddie had been very bold.

But he was bold, and stronger than you would think. For one thing, he never felt the heat; some coldness in his fair skin resisted it. He didn't burn red or brown, he didn't freckle much.

Hot days seemed to make him feel especially energetic. 'Now we'll run twice round the lawn and then you can pretend you're dying of thirst in the desert and that I'm an Arab chieftain bringing you water.'

'You must drink slowly,' he would say, 'for if you're very thirsty and you drink quickly you die.'

So I learnt the voluptuousness of drinking slowly when you are very thirsty – small mouthful by small mouthful, until the glass of pink, iced Coca-Cola was empty.

Just after my twelfth birthday Mr Sawyer died suddenly, and as Eddie's special friend I went to the funeral, wearing a new white dress. My straight hair was damped with sugar and water the night before and plaited into tight little plaits, so that it should be fluffy for the occasion.

When it was all over everybody said how nice Mrs Sawyer had looked, walking like a queen behind the coffin and crying her eyeballs out at the right moment, and wasn't Eddie a funny boy? He hadn't cried at all.

After this Eddie and I took possession of the room with the books. No one else ever entered it, except Mildred to sweep and dust in the mornings, and gradually the ghost of Mr Sawyer pulling Mrs Sawyer's hair faded though this took a little time. The blinds were always half-way down and going in out of the sun was like stepping into a pool of brown-green water. It was empty except for the bookshelves, a desk with a green baize top and a wicker rocking-chair.

'My room,' Eddie called it. 'My books,' he would say, 'my books.'

I don't know how long this lasted. I don't know whether it was weeks after Mr Sawyer's death or months after, that I see myself and Eddie in the room. But there we are and there, unexpectedly, are Mrs Sawyer and Mildred. Mrs Sawyer's mouth tight, her eyes pleased. She is pulling all the books out of the shelves and piling them into two heaps. The big, fat glossy ones – the good-looking ones, Mildred explains in a whisper – lie in one heap. The *Encyclopaedia Britannica*, *British Flowers, Birds and Beasts*, various histories, books with maps, Froude's *English in the West Indies* and so on – they are going to be sold. The unimportant books, with paper covers or damaged covers or torn pages, lie in another heap. They are going to be burnt – yes, burnt.

Mildred's expression was extraordinary as she said that – half hugely delighted, half-shocked, even frightened. And as for Mrs Sawyer – well, I knew bad temper (I had often seen it), I knew rage, but this was hate. I recognized the difference at once and stared at her curiously. I edged closer to her so that I could see the titles of the books she was handling.

It was the poetry shelf. *Poems*, Lord Byron, *Poetical Works*, Milton, and so on. Vlung, vlung, vlung – all thrown into the heap that were to be sold. But a book by Christina Rossetti, though also bound in leather, went into the heap that was to be burnt, and by a flicker in Mrs Sawyer's eyes I knew that worse than men who wrote books were women who wrote books –

infinitely worse. Men could be mercifully shot; women must be tortured.

Mrs Sawyer did not seem to notice that we were there, but she was breathing free and easy and her hands had got the rhythm of tearing and pitching. She looked beautiful, too – beautiful as the sky outside which was a very dark blue, or the mango tree, long sprays of brown and gold.

When Eddie said 'No', she did not even glance at him.

'No,' he said again in a high voice. 'Not that one. I was reading that one.'

She laughed and he rushed at her, his eyes starting out of his head, shrieking, 'Now I've got to hate you too. Now I hate you too.'

He snatched the book out of her hand and gave her a violent push. She fell into the rocking-chair.

Well, I wasn't going to be left out of all this, so I grabbed a book from the condemned pile and dived under Mildred's outstretched arm.

Then we were both in the garden. We ran along the path, bordered with crotons. We pelted down the path, though they did not follow us and we could hear Mildred laughing – kyah, kyah, kyah, kyah. As I ran I put the book I had taken into the loose front of my brown holland dress. It felt warm and alive.

When we got into the street we walked sedately, for we feared the black children's ridicule. I felt very happy, because I had saved this book and it was my book and I would read it from the beginning to the triumphant words 'The End'. But I was uneasy when I thought of Mrs Sawyer.

'What will she do?' I said.

'Nothing,' Eddie said. 'Not to me.'

He was white as a ghost in his sailor suit, a blue-white even in the setting sun, and his father's sneer was clamped on his face.

'But she'll tell your mother all sorts of lies about you,' he said. 'She's an awful liar. She can't make up a story to save her life, but she makes up lies about people all right.'

'My mother won't take any notice of her.' I said. Though I was not at all sure.

'Why not? Because she's…because she isn't white?'

Well, I knew the answer to that one. Whenever the subject

was brought up – people's relations and whether they had a drop of coloured blood or whether they hadn't – my father would grow impatient and interrupt. 'Who's white?' he would say. 'Damned few.'

So *I* said, 'Who's white? Damned few.'

'You can go to the devil,' Eddie said. 'She's prettier than your mother. When she's asleep her mouth smiles and she has curling eyelashes and quantities and quantities and *quantities* of hair.'

'Yes,' I said truthfully. 'She's prettier than my mother.'

It was a red sunset that evening, a huge, sad, frightening sunset.

'Look, let's go back,' I said. 'If you're sure she won't be vexed with you, let's go back. It'll be dark soon.'

At his gate he asked me not to go. 'Don't go yet, don't go yet.'

We sat under the mango tree and I was holding his hand when he began to cry. Drops fell on my hand like the water from the dripstone in the filter in our yard. Then I began to cry too and when I felt my own tears on my hand I thought, 'Now perhaps we're married.'

'Yes, certainly, now we're married,' I thought. But I didn't say anything. I didn't say a thing until I was sure he had stopped. Then I asked, 'What's your book?'

'It's *Kim*,' he said. 'But it got torn. It starts at page twenty now. What's the one you took?'

'I don't know; it's too dark to see,' I said.

When I got home I rushed into my bedroom and locked the door because I knew that this book was the most important thing that had ever happened to me and I did not want anybody to be there when I looked at it.

But I was very disappointed, because it was in French and seemed dull. *Fort Comme La Mort*, it was called....

Pioneers, Oh, Pioneers

As the two girls were walking up yellow-hot Market Street, Irene nudged her sister and said: 'Look at her!'

They were not far from the market, they could still smell the fish.

When Rosalie turned her head the few white women she saw carried parasols. The black women were barefooted, wore gaily striped turbans and highwaisted dresses. It was still the nineteenth century, November 1899.

'There she goes,' said Irene.

And there was Mrs Menzies, riding up to her house on the Morne for a cool weekend.

'Good morning,' Rosalie said, but Mrs Menzies did not answer. She rode past, clip-clop, clip-clop, in her thick, dark riding habit brought from England ten years before, balancing a large dripping parcel wrapped in flannel on her knee.

'It's ice. She wants her drinks cold,' said Rosalie.

'Why can't she have it sent up like everybody else? The black people laugh at her. She ought to be ashamed of herself.'

'I don't see why,' Rosalie said obstinately.

'Oh, you,' Irene jeered. 'You like crazy people. You like Jimmy Longa and you like old maman Menzies. You liked Ramage, nasty beastly horrible Ramage.'

Rosalie said: 'You cried about him yesterday.'

'Yesterday doesn't count. Mother says we were all hysterical yesterday.'

By this time they were nearly home so Rosalie said nothing. But she put her tongue out as they went up the steps into the long, cool gallery.

Their father, Dr Cox, was sitting in an armchair with a three-legged table by his side.

On the table were his pipe, his tin of tobacco and his glasses. Also *The Times* weekly edition, the *Cornhill Magazine*, the *Lancet* and a West Indian newspaper, the *Dominica Herald and Leeward Islands Gazette*.

He was not to be spoken to, as they saw at once though one was only eleven and the other nine.

'Dead as a door nail,' he muttered as they went past him into the next room so comfortably full of rocking chairs, a mahogany table, palm leaf fans, a tigerskin rug, family photographs, view of Bettws-y-Coed and a large picture of wounded soldiers in the snow, Napoleon's Retreat from Moscow.

The doctor had not noticed his daughters, for he too was thinking about Mr Ramage. He had liked the man, stuck up for him, laughed off his obvious eccentricities, denied point blank that he was certifiable. All wrong. Ramage, probably a lunatic, was now as dead as a door nail. Nothing to be done.

Ramage had first arrived in the island two years before, a handsome man in tropical kit, white suit, red cummerbund, solar topee. After he grew tired of being followed about by an admiring crowd of negro boys he stopped wearing the red sash and the solar topee but he clung to his white suits though most of the men wore dark trousers even when the temperature was ninety in the shade.

Miss Lambton, who had been a fellow passenger from Barbados, reported that he was certainly a gentleman and also a king among men when it came to looks. But he was very unsociable. He ignored all invitations to dances, tennis parties and moonlight picnics. He never went to church and was not to be seen at the club. He seemed to like Dr Cox, however, and dined with him one evening. And Rosalie, then aged seven, fell in love.

After dinner, though the children were not supposed to talk much when guests were there, and were usually not allowed downstairs at all, she edged up to him and said: 'Sing something.' (People who came to dinner often sang afterwards, as she well knew.)

'I can't sing,' said Ramage.

'Yes you can.' Her mother's disapproving expression made

her insist the more. 'You can. You can.'

He laughed and hoisted her on to his knee. With her head against his chest she listened while he rumbled gently: 'Baa baa black sheep, have you any wool? Yes sir, yes sir, three bags full.'

Then the gun at the fort fired for nine o'clock and the girls, smug in their stiff white dresses, had to say goodnight nicely and go upstairs to bed.

After a perfunctory rubber of whist with a dummy, Mrs Cox also departed. Over his whisky and soda Ramage explained that he'd come to the island with the intention of buying an estate. 'Small, and as remote as possible.'

'That won't be difficult here.'

'So I heard,' said Ramage.

'Tried any of the other islands?'

'I went to Barbados first.'

'Little England,' the doctor said. 'Well?'

'I was told that there were several places going along this new Imperial Road you've got here.'

'Won't last,' Dr Cox said. 'Nothing lasts in this island. Nothing will come of it. You'll see.'

Ramage looked puzzled.

'It's all a matter of what you want the place for,' the doctor said without explaining himself. 'Are you after a good interest on your capital or what?'

'Peace,' Ramage said. 'Peace, that's what I'm after.'

'You'll have to pay for that,' the doctor said.

'What's the price?' said Ramage, smiling. He put one leg over the other. His bare ankle was hairy and thin, his hands long and slender for such a big man.

'You'll be very much alone.'

'That will suit me,' Ramage said.

'And if you're far along the road, you'll have to cut the trees down, burn the stumps and start from scratch.'

'Isn't there a half-way house?' Ramage said.

The doctor answered rather vaguely: 'You might be able to get hold of one of the older places.'

He was thinking of young Errington, of young Kellaway, who had both bought estates along the Imperial Road and worked hard. But they had given up after a year or two, sold their land cheap and gone back to England. They could not stand the loneliness and melancholy of the forest.

A fortnight afterwards Miss Lambton told Mrs Cox that Mr Ramage had bought Spanish Castle, the last but one of the older properties. It was beautiful but not prosperous – some said bad luck, others bad management. His nearest neighbour was Mr Eliot, who owned *Malgré Tout*. Now called Twickenham.

For several months after this Ramage disappeared and one afternoon at croquet Mrs Cox asked Miss Lambton if she had any news of him.

'A strange man,' she said, 'very reserved.'

'Not so reserved as all that, said Miss Lambton. 'He got married several weeks ago. He told me that he didn't want it talked about.'

'No!' said Mrs Cox. 'Who to?'

Then it all came out. Ramage had married a coloured girl who called herself Isla Harrison, though she had no right to the name of Harrison. Her mother was dead and she'd been brought up by her godmother, old Miss Myra, according to local custom. Miss Myra kept a sweetshop in Bay Street and Isla was very well known in the town – too well known.

'He took her to Trinidad,' said Miss Lambton mournfully, 'and when they came back they were married. They went down to Spanish Castle and I've heard nothing about them since.'

'It's not as though she was a nice coloured girl,' everybody said.

So the Ramages were lost to white society. Lost to everyone but Dr Cox. Spanish Castle estate was in a district which he visited every month, and one afternoon as he was driving past he saw Ramage standing near his letter box which was nailed to a tree visible from the road. He waved. Ramage waved back and beckoned.

While they were drinking punch on the verandah, Mrs Ramage came in. She was dressed up to the nines, smelt very strongly of cheap scent and talked loudly in an aggressive voice. No, she certainly wasn't a nice coloured girl.

The doctor tried – too hard perhaps – for the next time he

called at Spanish Castle a door banged loudly inside the house and a grinning boy told him that Mr Ramage was out.

'And Mrs Ramage?'

'The mistress is not at home.'

At the end of the path the doctor looked back and saw her at a window peering at him.

He shook his head, but he never went there again, and the Ramage couple sank out of sight, out of mind.

It was Mr Eliot, the owner of Twickenham, who started the trouble. He was out with his wife, he related, looking at some young nutmeg trees near the boundary. They had a boy with them who had lighted a fire and put on water for tea. They looked up and saw Ramage coming out from under the trees. He was burnt a deep brown, his hair fell to his shoulders, his beard to his chest. He was wearing sandals and a leather belt, on one side of which hung a cutlass, on the other a large pouch. Nothing else.

'If,' said Mr Eliot, 'the man had apologized to my wife, if he'd shown the slightest consciousness of the fact that he was stark naked, I would have overlooked the whole thing. God knows one learns to be tolerant in this wretched place. But not a bit of it. He stared hard at her and came out with: 'What an uncomfortable dress – and how ugly!' My wife got very red. Then she said: "Mr Ramage, the kettle is just boiling. Will you have some tea?"'

'Good for her,' said the doctor. 'What did he say to that?'

'Well, he seemed rather confused. He bowed from the waist, exactly as if he had clothes on, and explained that he never drank tea. "I have a stupid habit of talking to myself. I beg your pardon," he said, and off he went. We got home and my wife locked herself in the bedroom. When she came out she wouldn't speak to me at first, then she said that he was quite right, I didn't care what she looked like, so now she didn't either. She called me a mean man. A mean man. I won't have it,' said Mr Eliot indignantly. 'He's mad, walking about with a cutlass. He's dangerous.'

'Oh, I don't think so,' said Dr Cox. 'He'd probably left his clothes round the corner and didn't know how to explain. Perhaps we do cover ourselves up too much. The sun can be

good for you. The best thing in the world. If you'd seen as I
have....'

Mr Eliot interrupted at once. He knew that when the doctor
started talking about his unorthodox methods he went on for a
long time.

'I don't know about all that. But I may as well tell you that I
dislike the idea of a naked man with a cutlass wandering about
near my place. I dislike it very much indeed. I've got to
consider my wife and my daughter. Something ought to be
done.'

Eliot told his story to everyone who'd listen and the
Ramages became the chief topic of conversation.

'It seems,' Mrs Cox told her husband, 'that he does wear a
pair of trousers as a rule and even an old coat when it rains, but
several people have watched him lying in a hammock on the
verandah naked. You ought to call there and speak to him.
They say,' she added, 'that the two of them fight like Kilkenny
cats. He's making himself very unpopular.'

So the next time he visited the district Dr Cox stopped near
Spanish Castle. As he went up the garden path he noticed how
unkempt and deserted the place looked. The grass on the lawn
had grown very high and the verandah hadn't been swept for
days.

The doctor paused uncertainly, then tapped on the sitting-
room door, which was open. 'Hallo,' called Ramage from
inside the house, and he appeared, smiling. He was wearing
one of his linen suits, clean and pressed, and his hair and
beard were trimmed.

'You're looking very well,' the doctor said.

'Oh, yes, I feel splendid. Sit down and I'll get you a drink.'

There seemed to be no one else in the house.

'The servants have all walked out,' Ramage explained when
he appeared with the punch.

'Good Lord, have they?'

'Yes, but I think I've found an old woman in the village
who'll come up and cook.'

'And how is Mrs Ramage?'

At this moment there was a heavy thud on the side of the
house, then another, then another.

'What was that?' asked Dr Cox.

'Somebody throwing stones. They do sometimes.'

'Why, in heaven's name?'

'I don't know. Ask them.'

Then the doctor repeated Eliot's story, but in spite of himself it came out as trivial, even jocular.

'Yes, I was very sorry about that,' Ramage answered casually. 'They startled me as much as I startled them. I wasn't expecting to see anyone. It was a bit of bad luck but it won't happen again.'

'It was bad luck meeting Eliot,' the doctor said.

And that was the end of it. When he got up to go, no advice, no warning had been given.

'You're sure you're all right here?'

'Yes, of course,' said Ramage.

'It's all rubbish,' the doctor told his wife that evening. 'The man's as fit as a fiddle, nothing wrong with him at all.'

'Was Mrs Ramage there?'

'No, thank God. She was out.'

'I hear this morning,' said Mrs Cox, 'that she's disappeared. Hasn't been seen for weeks.'

The doctor laughed heartily. 'Why can't they leave those two alone? What rubbish!'

'Well,' said Mrs Cox without smiling, 'it's odd, isn't it?'

'Rubbish,' the doctor said again some days later, for, spurred on by Mr Eliot, people were talking venomously and he could not stop them. Mrs Ramage was not at Spanish Castle, she was not in the town. Where was she?

Old Myra was questioned. She said that she had not seen her god-daughter and had not heard from her 'since long time'. The Inspector of Police had two anonymous letters – the first writer claimed to know 'all what happen at Spanish Castle one night': the other said that witnesses were frightened to come forward and speak against a white man.

The *Gazette* published a fiery article:

'The so-called "Imperial Road" was meant to attract young Englishmen with capital who would buy and develop properties in the interior. This costly experiment has not been a success, and one of the last of these gentlemen planters has seen himself as the king of the cannibal islands ever since he landed. We have it, on the best authority, that his very eccentric behaviour has been the greatest possible annoyance to his neighbour. Now the whole thing has become much more serious....'

It ended: 'Black people bear much; must they also bear beastly murder and nothing done about it?'

'You don't suppose that I believe all these lies, do you?' Dr Cox told Mr Eliot, and Mr Eliot answered: 'Then I'll make it my business to find out the truth. That man is a menace, as I said from the first, and he should be dealt with.'

'Dear Ramage,' Dr Cox wrote. 'I'm sorry to tell you that stupid and harmful rumours are being spread about your wife and yourself. I need hardly say that no one with a grain of sense takes them seriously, but people here are excitable and very ready to believe mischiefmakers, so I strongly advise you to put a stop to the talk at once and to take legal action if necessary.'

But the doctor got no answer to this letter, for in the morning news reached the town of a riot at Spanish Castle the night before.

A crowd of young men and boys, and a few women, had gone up to Ramage's house to throw stones. It was a bright moonlight night. He had come on to the verandah and stood there facing them. He was dressed in white and looked very tall, they said, like a zombi. He said something that nobody heard, a man shouted 'white zombi' and thrown a stone which hit him. He went into the house and came out with a shotgun. Then stories differed wildly. He had fired and hit a woman in the front of the crowd.... No, he'd hit a little boy at the back.... He hadn't fired at all, but had threatened them. It was agreed that in the rush to get away people had been knocked down and hurt, one woman seriously.

It was also rumoured that men and boys from the village planned to burn down Spanish Castle house, if possible with Ramage inside. After this there was no more hesitation. The next day a procession walked up the garden path to the house – the Inspector of Police, three policemen and Dr Cox.

'He must give some explanation of all this', said the Inspector.

The doors and windows were all open, and they found Ramage and the shotgun, but they got no explanation. He had been dead for some hours.

His funeral was an impressive sight. A good many came out of
curiosity, a good many because, though his death was said to
be 'an accident', they felt guilty. For behind the coffin walked
Mrs Ramage, sent for post-haste by old Myra. She'd been
staying with relatives in Guadeloupe. When asked why she
had left so secretly – she had taken a fishing boat from the
other side of the island – she answered sullenly that she didn't
want anyone to know her business, she knew how people
talked. No, she'd heard no rumours about her husband, and
the *Gazette* – a paper written in English – was not read in
Guadeloupe.

'Eh-eh,' echoed Myra. 'Since when the girl obliged to tell
everybody where she go and what she do chapter and
verse….'

It was lovely weather, and on their way to the Anglican
cemetery many had tears in their eyes.

But already public opinion was turning against Ramage.

'His death was really a blessing in disguise', said one lady.
'He was evidently mad, poor man – sitting in the sun with no
clothes on – much worse might have happened.'

'This is All Souls Day,' Rosalie thought, standing at her
bedroom window before going to sleep. She was wishing that
Mr Ramage could have been buried in the Catholic cemetery,
where all day the candles burnt almost invisible in the
sunlight. When night came they twinkled like fire-flies. The
graves were covered with flowers – some real, some red or
yellow paper or little gold cut-outs. Sometimes there was a
letter weighted by a stone and the black people said that next
morning the letters had gone. And where? Who would steal
letters on the night of the dead? But the letters had gone.

The Anglican cemetery, which was not very far away, down
the hill, was deserted and silent. Protestants believed that
when you were dead, you were dead.

If he had a letter…she thought.

'My dear darling Mr Ramage,' she wrote, then felt so sad
that she began to cry.

Two hours later Mrs Cox came into the room and found her

daughter in bed and asleep; on the table by her side was the unfinished letter. Mrs Cox read it, frowned, pressed her lips together, then crumpled it up and threw it out of the window.

There was a stiff breeze and she watched it bouncing purposefully down the street. As if it knew exactly where it was going.

Goodbye Marcus,
Goodbye Rose

'When first I wore my old shako,' sang Captain Cardew, 'Ten, twenty, thirty, forty, fifty years ago...' and Phoebe thought what a wonderful bass voice he had. This was the second time he had called to take her for a walk, and again he had brought her a large box of chocolates.

Captain Cardew and his wife were spending the winter in Jamaica when they visited the small island where she lived and found it so attractive and unspoilt that they decided to stay. They even talked of buying a house and settling there for good.

He was not only a very handsome old man but a hero who had fought bravely in some long ago war which she thought you only read about in history books. He's been wounded and had a serious operation without an anaesthetic. Anaesthetics weren't invented in those days. (Better not think too much about that.)

It had been impressed on her how kind it was of him to bother with a little girl like herself. Anyway she liked him, he was always so carefully polite to her, treating her as though she were a grown-up girl. A calm unruffled man, he only grew annoyed if people called him 'Captain' too often. Sometimes he lost his temper and would say loudly things like: 'What d'you think I'm Captain of now – a Penny a Liner?' What was a Penny a Liner? She never found out.

It was a lovely afternoon and they set out. She was wearing a white blouse with a sailor collar, a long full white skirt, black stockings, black buttoned boots and a large wide-brimmed white hat anchored firmly with elastic under her chin.

When they reached the Botanical Gardens she offered to take him to a shady bench and they walked slowly to the secluded part of the Gardens that she'd spoken of and sat under a large tree. Beyond its shadow they could see the yellow dancing patches of sunlight.

'Do you mind if I take off my hat? The elastic is hurting me,' Phoebe said.

'Then take it off, take it off,' said the Captain.

Phoebe took off her hat and began to talk in what she hoped was a grown-up way about the curator, Mr Harcourt-Smith, who'd really made the Gardens as beautiful as they were. He'd come from a place in England called the Kew. Had he ever heard of it?

Yes he had heard of it. He added: 'How old are you Phoebe?'

'I'm twelve,' said Phoebe, '– and a bit.'

'Hah!' said the Captain. 'Then soon you'll be old enough to have a lover!' His hand, which had been lying quietly by his side, darted towards her, dived inside her blouse and clamped itself around one very small breast. 'Quite old enough,' he remarked.

Phoebe remained perfectly still. 'He's making a great mistake, a great mistake,' she thought. 'If I don't move he'll take his hand away without really noticing what he's done.'

However the Captain showed no sign of that at all. He was breathing rather heavily when a couple came strolling round the corner. Calmly, without hurry, he withdrew his hand and after a while said: 'Perhaps we ought to be going home now.'

Phoebe, who was in a ferment, said nothing. They walked out of the shade into the sun and as they walked she looked up at him as though at some aged but ageless god. He talked of usual things in a usual voice and she made up her mind that she would tell nobody of what had happened. Nobody. It was not a thing you could possibly talk about. Also no one would believe exactly how it had happened, and whether they believed her or not she would be blamed.

If he was as absentminded as all that – for surely it could be nothing but absentmindedness – perhaps there oughtn't to be any more walks. She could excuse herself by saying that she had a headache. But that would only do for once. The walks continued. They'd go into the Gardens or up the Morne, a hill overlooking the town. There were benches and seats there but few houses and hardly anybody about.

He never touched her again but all through the long bright afternoons Captain Cardew talked of love and Phoebe listened, shocked and fascinated. Sometimes she doubted what he said: surely it was impossible, horrifyingly impossible. Sometimes she was on the point of saying, not 'You oughtn't to talk to me like this' but babyishly 'I want to go home.' He always knew when she felt this and would at once change the subject and tell her amusing stories of his life when he was a young man and a subaltern in India.

'Hot?' he'd say. 'This isn't hot. India's hot. Sometimes the only thing to do is take off your clothes and see that the punkah's going.'

Or he'd talk about London long ago. Someone – was it Byron? – had said that women were never so unattractive as when they were eating and it was still most unfashionable for them to eat heartily. He'd watch in wonder as the ethereal creatures pecked daintily, then sent away almost untouched plates. One day he had seen a maid taking a tray laden with food up to the bedrooms and the mystery was explained.

But these stories were only intervals in the ceaseless talk of love, various ways of making love, various sorts of love. He'd explain that love was not kind and gentle, as she had imagined, but violent. Violence, even cruelty, was an essential part of it. He would expand on this, it seemed to be his favourite subject.

The walks had gone on for some time when the Captain's wife, Edith, who was a good deal younger than her husband, became suspicious and began making very sarcastic remarks. Early one evening when the entire party had gone up the Morne to watch the sunset, she'd said to her husband, after a long look at Phoebe: 'Do you really find the game worth the candle?' Captain Cardew said nothing. He watched the sun going down without expression, then remarked that it was quite true that the only way to get rid of a temptation was to yield to it.

Phoebe had never liked Edith very much. Now she began to dislike her. One afternoon they were in a room together and she said: 'Do you see how white my hair's becoming? It's all because of you.' And when Phoebe answered truthfully that she didn't notice any white hairs: 'What a really dreadful little liar you are!'

After this she must have spoken to Phoebe's mother, a silent, reserved woman, who said nothing to her daughter but began to watch her in a puzzled, incredulous, even faintly suspicious way. Phoebe knew that very soon she would be questioned, she'd have to explain.

So she was more than half relieved when Edith Cardew announced that they'd quite given up their first idea of spending the rest of the winter on the island and were going back to England by the next boat. When Captain Cardew said 'Goodbye' formally, the evening before they left, she had smiled and shaken hands, not quite realizing that she was very unlikely ever to see him again.

There was a flat roof outside her bedroom window. On hot fine nights she'd often lie there in her nightgown looking up at the huge brilliant stars. She'd once tried to write a poem about them but had not got beyond the first line: 'My stars. Familiar jewels.' But that night she knew that she would never finish it. They were not jewels. They were not familiar. They were cold, infinitely far away, quite indifferent.

The roof looked onto the yard and she could hear Victoria and Joseph talking and laughing outside the pantry, then they must have gone away and it was quite silent. She was alone in the house for she'd not gone with the others to see the Cardews off. She was sure that now they had gone her mother would be very unlikely to question her, and then began to wonder how he had been so sure, not only that she'd never tell anybody but that she'd make no effort at all to stop him talking. That could only mean that he'd seen at once that she was not a good girl – who would object – but a wicked one – who would listen. He must know. He knew. It was so.

It was so and she felt not so much unhappy about this as uncomfortable, even dismayed. It was like wearing a dress that was much too big for her, a dress that swallowed her up.

Wasn't it quite difficult being a wicked girl? Even more difficult than being a good one? Besides, didn't the nuns say that Chastity, in Thought, Word and Deed was your most precious possession? She remembered Mother Sacred Heart, her second favourite, reciting in her lovely English voice: 'So dear to Heaven is saintly chastity....' How did it go on? Something about 'a thousand liveried angels lackey her....'

'A thousand liveried angels' now no more. The thought of some vague irreparable loss saddened her. Then she told herself that anyway she needn't bother any longer about whether she'd get married or not. The older girls that she knew talked a great deal about marriage, some of them talked about very little else. And they seemed so sure. No sooner had they put their hair up and begun going to dances, than they'd marry someone handsome (and rich). Then the fun of being grown-up and important, of doing what you wanted instead of what you were told to do, would start. And go on for a long long time.

But she'd always doubted if this would happen to her. Even if numbers of rich and handsome young men suddenly appeared, would she be one of the chosen?

> If no one ever marries me
> And I don't see why they should
> For nurse says I'm not pretty
> And I'm seldom very good...

That was it exactly.

Well there was one thing. Now she felt very wise, very grown-up, she could forget these childish worries. She could hardly believe that only a few weeks ago she, like all the others, had secretly made lists of her trousseau, decided on the names of her three children. Jack. Marcus. And Rose.

Now goodbye Marcus, goodbye Rose. The prospect before her might be difficult and uncertain but it was far more exciting.

Overture and Beginners Please

We were sitting by the fire in the small dining-room when Camilla said 'I hate my parents, don't you?' Hail was rattling against the curtained windows. I had been told all about snow long before I left the West Indies, hail was a surprise and exciting in its way. I though I'd be laughed at if I asked what it was.

Another dark yellow curtain hung over the door which led into a passage and beyond that were the empty classrooms, for this was the week after Christmas and the day girls and seven other boarders had gone home for their holidays.

'And what's more,' said Camilla, 'they hate me. They like my younger sister. A lot of that sort of thing goes on in families but it's hushed up of course.'

It was almost dark, I was almost warm, so I said, 'I don't hate mine. They gave a farewell dance for me before I left. We had a band. It's funny, I can remember exactly the face of the man with the shak-shak.'

'How comic,' said Camilla who seemed annoyed.

'They play well. Different music of course.'

'Why did they send you to the old Perse if they were so fond of you?'

'Because my English aunt said it was a good school.'

'That's the one who won't have you with her for Christmas, isn't it?'

'Well she is sick – ill, I mean.'

'*She says*! How do you like it now you are here?'

'I like it all right, but the chilblains on my hands hurt.'

Then she said I would have lots of time to find out if I did like it as she was leaving the next day to stay with friends at Thaxted. 'Miss Born has all of Charlotte M. Yonge's novels lined up for you to read in the evenings.'

'Oh Lord, she hasn't!'

'Just you wait,' said Camilla.

The maid came in to light up and soon it would be time to go upstairs and change for dinner. I thought this woman one of the most fascinating I had ever seen. She had a long thin face, dead white, or powdered dead white. Her hair was black and lively under her cap, her eyes so small that the first time I saw her I thought she was blind. But wide open, they were the most astonishing blue, cornflower blue, no, more like sparks of blue fire. Then she would drop her eyelids and her face would go dead and lifeless again. I never tired of watching this transformation.

After dinner there I was, reading aloud *The Dove in the Eagle's Nest*. Camilla didn't listen, nor did Miss Rode, our headmistress, who was a middle-aged very imposing woman with quantities of black-grey hair arranged like a coronet. She dressed in various shades of brown, purple, puce or mustard and her face was serene and kind.

Miss Born however never took her eyes off me. Miss Born was old, she wore black, she never taught. She represented breeding and culture and was a great asset to the school. 'Drop your voice,' she would say, 'drop it. An octave at least'; or 'That will do, don't go on, I really cannot bear any more tonight.'

We sat around the fire till the clock struck nine. 'Goodnight Miss Rode.' 'Goodnight, dear child' said Miss Rode, who was wearing her purple, always a good sign. 'Goodnight Miss Born.' Miss Born inclined her head very slightly and as I went out remarked, 'Why did you insist on that girl playing Autolycus? Tony Lumpkin in person.'

'Not in person, surely,' said Miss Rode mildly.

'In manner then, in manner,' said Miss Born.

Camilla shut the door and I heard no more.

The staircase was slippery and smelt of floor polish. All the way up to the bedroom floor I thought about Miss Born's black clothes, her small active body. A mouse with a parrot's head. I hadn't even wanted to be in the old *Winter's Tale* and I told them so. However, I said nothing of all this to Camilla for I had been five months in England and was slowly learning to be cautious. Besides the bedrooms were unheated and I had already begun to shiver and shake.

'Don't you think it's frightfully cold, Camilla?'

'No, not particularly. Hop into bed and you'll soon get warm.' She went off to her own room four doors away.

I knew of course that I would not sleep or get warm for on top of everything else an icy wind was blowing through the window, which for some mysterious reason must be left open six inches at the top.

Do not shut your window. This window must not be closed.

I was still awake and shivering, clutching my ankles with my hands, when the maid, who was called Jarvis, knocked. 'I've brought you up a hot water bottle miss.'

'Oh thank you. How awfully kind of you.'

'It is my own hot water bottle,' she said. She asked why I didn't shut my window.

'Well, I though we weren't supposed to.'

She pushed the sash up without answering. I stretched my legs out and put the bottle where my back hurt and thanked her again. I hoped she'd go away but she lingered.

'I wanted to tell you miss, that I enjoyed the school play this term very much. You were good in that boy's part.'

'Autolycus.'

'Well, I don't remember the name but you quite cheered me up.'

'I'm very glad,' I said. 'Goodnight Jarvis, don't catch cold in this icy little room.'

'I had a great success once in an amateur theatrical performance,' she went on dreamily. 'I played the part of a blind girl.'

'You played a blind girl? How strange, because when I saw you first I thought....' I stopped. 'I thought you might be able to act because you don't look at all wooden.'

'The flowers I had sent me,' she said. 'Roses and that. Of course, it was long ago, when I was a girl, but I still remember my part, every word of it.'

'How very nice' was all I could think of to say. She snapped the light out and shut the door, rather loudly.

She played a blind girl. I thought she was blind. But this sort of thing had happened to me before. I'd stopped trying to make sense of clues that led nowhere.

When, next day after breakfast, Camilla left I got through the morning thinking no bicycle ride anyhow. Patey isn't here.

Miss Patey had been trying to teach me to bicycle. She always skimmed gracefully ahead as though she had nothing to do with me and I followed her, wobbling dangerously from side to side. Once when I'd fallen into a ditch on the way to Newnham, she turned back and asked in a detached way if I'd hurt myself. 'Oh no, Miss Patey, not at all.' I climbed out of the ditch and picked up the bicycle. 'I see your stocking is torn and that is quite a bruise on your knee.' She did not speak again until we got to the Trumpington Road. 'You had better get down and wheel your bicycle here.' 'Yes, Miss Patey.'

Limping along the Trumpington Road…past Mrs G's house, a distant relative of my father's. I was allowed to have tea with her every Saturday afternoon…. She was called Jeanette and was a very lovely, stately old lady with thick white hair, huge black eyes and a classic profile. She didn't wear spectacles except for reading and her hands were slender and transparent looking. She talked about Cambridge when she was young and the famous men she'd known. 'Poor Darwin. He threaded the labyrinths of creation and lost his Creator.' Or 'Of course Fitzgerald's translation from the Persian was not really accurate…'; and the Song of Solomon was an allegory of Christ and His Church.

Another day she told me that she had nearly eloped (tired of her absent-minded old husband, I suppose). She was packed and ready to leave but when she was pinning on her hat she saw in the looking-glass the devil grinning over her shoulder. She was so frightened that she changed her mind.

'And what did the devil look like?' I asked, very curious. But she never told me that.

Like so many beautiful old ladies then she had a devoted maid whom I was rather afraid of, she looked at me so sternly, so unsmilingly when she opened the door. Now I come to think of it, Jarvis didn't smile either.

None of the girls could believe that I'd never owned a bicycle

before or that there were very few in the island. 'How do you
get about then, if there are no trains, buses, cars or bicycles?'
they would say. 'Horses, mules, carriages, buggies, traps.'
Winks, smiles. 'Is it "honey don't try so hard" or "honey don't
cry so hard"?' 'How should I know?' 'Well, it's a coon song,
you ought to know.' But when I discovered that though they
never believed the truth, they swallowed the most fantastic
lies, I amused myself a good deal.

That first afternoon when I had walked along the gravel path
which circled the muddy green hockey field, I crossed a flower
bed and looked into one of the dim classrooms. It was a
grey-yellow day. Not so bad as the white glaring days or the
icy wind days. Still, bad enough. The sky was the colour of no
hope, but they don't notice it, they are used to it, they expect
me to grow used to it.

It was while I was staring at the empty ghostly-looking
desks that I felt a lump in my throat. Tears – my heart a heavy
jagged weight. Of course premonitions, presentiments had
brushed me before, cold and clammy as a bat's wing, but
nothing like this. Despair, grey-yellow like their sky. I stayed
by the window in the cold thinking 'What is going to become of
me? Why am I here at all?'

One hot silent July afternoon I was told that I was to go to
England with my Aunt Clare, who had been staying with us
for the last six months. I was to go to a school called The Perse
in Cambridge.

'It is very good of her to take charge of you.' I noticed that my
father was looking at me in a critical, disapproving way. 'I am
sure,' he said, 'that it will do you a great deal of good.'

'I sincerely hope so,' said Aunt Clare dubiously.

This interview chilled me and I was silent all that evening.
(So, I noticed, was my mother.) I went up to my bedroom early
and took out the exercise book that I called 'Secret Poems.'

I am going to England
What shall I find there?

'No matter what
Not what I sought' said Byron.

Not what I sought,

Not what I seek.

I wrote no more poems for a very long time.

Unfortunately it was a grey lowering August in London, not cold but never bright or fresh. My Aunt Clare, a tireless walker, dragged me round to see all the sights and after a week I went to sleep in the most unlikely places; St Paul's, Westminster Abbey, Madame Tussaud's, the Wallace Collection, the zoo, even a shop or two. She was a swift but absentminded walker and I could easily lag behind and find a chair or bench to droop on.

'She can't help it,' I heard her explain once. 'It's the change of climate, but it can really be very annoying.'

Mistake after mistake.

But I knew the exact day when I lost belief in myself and cold caution took control. It was when she bought me the ugly dress instead of the pretty wine-coloured one.

'It's a perfect fit,' said the saleswoman, 'and the young lady is so pale, she needs colour.'

My aunt looked at the price ticket. 'No, not at all suitable,' she said and chose a drab dress which I disliked. I didn't argue for the big shop and the saleswoman whom I thought very beautiful bewildered me. But I was heartbroken. I'd have to appear before a lot of strange girls in this hideous garment. 'They're bound to dislike me.'

Outside in the hostile street we got into the hateful bus (always squashed up against perfect strangers – millions of perfect strangers in this horrible place). The bus wheels said 'And *when* we say we've *always* won, and *when* they ask us *how* it's done.' (You wouldn't dare say how you do it, not straight out you wouldn't it's too damned mean the way you do it.)

At Cambridge I refused to say anything except 'Oh yes, that's very nice indeed. This bridge, that building. King's College Chapel. Oh yes. Very nice.'

'Is that all you can say about King's College Chapel?' said Miss Born disdainfully.

Privately I thought that a Protestant service was all wrong in King's College Chapel, that it missed the smell of incense, splendid vestments, Latin prayers. 'You've forgotten that you stole it from the Catholics but it hasn't forgotten,' I thought. Fortunately I didn't say this.

'They sang very nicely indeed.'

Well, I walked up and down the hockey field till I'd stopped crying then went back to the small dining-room where there was always a blazing fire, I will say. But I could not eat anything and Miss Rode sent me to bed.

'I hear,' she said, 'that you feel the cold, so you'll find extra blankets and Jarvis will bring you up a hot water bottle and hot milk.'

Lying in bed, warm and comfortable, I tried to argue my fears away. After all, it's only for another eighteen months at the worst and though I don't particularly want to go back, there it is, solid and safe, the street, the sandbox tree, the stone steps, the long gallery with the round table at the top. But I was astonished to discover how patchy, vague and uncertain my memory had become. I had forgotten so much so soon.

I remembered the stars, but not the moon. It was a different moon, but different in what way? I didn't know. I remembered the shadows of trees more clearly than the trees, the sound of rain but not the sound of my mother's voice. Not really. I remembered the smell of dust and heat, the coolness of ferns but not the scent of any of the flowers. As for the mountains, the hills and the sea, they were not only thousands of miles away, they were years away.

About three days before the holidays ended, Miss Rode handed me a letter from Switzerland. 'But I don't know anyone in Switzerland.'

'Open it and find out,' she said.

I put the letter under my pillow for a time, thinking it would be something to look forward to the next morning, but I was too curious to wait. I opened it – it was signed Myrtle. I was disappointed. What on earth had Myrtle, a girl I hardly knew, to write to me about? This was the letter which was to change my life.

Dear West Indies,

I have been thinking about you a lot since I came to Switzerland, perhaps because my mother is getting divorced. I see now what a silly lot of fools we were about everything that matters and I don't think you are. It was all those words in *The Winter's Tale* that Miss Born wanted to blue pencil, you rolled them out as though you knew what they meant. My mother said you made the other girls look like waxworks and when you dropped your cap you picked it up so naturally, like a born actress. She says that you ought to go on the stage and why don't you? I like Switzerland all right. There are a lot of English here and my mother says what a pity! She can be very sarcastic. Let me hear from you soon. I felt I simply had to write this.

Yours ever,
Myrtle

I read this letter over and over again, then rolled about from side to side making up an answer. 'Dear Myrtle, Thanks for letter. I did not know what the words meant, I just liked the sound of them. I thought your mother very pretty, but yes, a bit sarky.'

Then I stopped writing the imaginary letter to Myrtle for suddenly, like an illumination, I knew exactly what I wanted to do. Next day I wrote to my father. I told him that I longed to be an actress and that I wanted to go to the Academy of Dramatic Art in Gower Street.

'I am *quite* sure. Please think very seriously about it. I don't mind this place and some of the mistresses are quite all right but it's really a waste of money my being here....'

When the answer arrived it was yes and I was happier than I'd ever been in my life. Nothing could touch me, not praise, nor blame. Nor incredulous smiles. A new term had started but Myrtle hadn't come back and Camilla was still away in Thaxted.

'There is an entrance examination,' they'd say. 'You won't pass it.'

'Yes I will,' but really I was extremely nervous about this examination and surprised when I did pass. The judges had seemed so very bored. The place was not Royal then and was known colloquially as 'Tree's School'. It wasn't so choosy then perhaps.

My aunt installed me in an Upper Bedford Place

boarding-house and left me to it; she strongly disapproved of the whole business. However she soon came back to London and took a small flat near Baker Street to see for herself how I was getting on.

'When you're stabbed in the back you fall like this, and when you're stabbed in front you fall like this, but if you stab yourself you fall differently. Like this.'

'Is that all you've learnt?'

'No.' I told her about fencing classes, ballet, elocution, gesture. And so on. 'No plays?' she wanted to know. 'Yes of course. I was Celia in *As You Like It* and we did Paolo and Francesca once.' And I was Francesca in the little dark sitting-room.

'"Now I am free and gay,
Light as a dancer when the strings begin
All ties that held me I cast off...."'

'You'll find that very expensive,' my aunt said.

I spent the vacation with relatives in Yorkshire and one morning early my uncle woke me with a cablegram of the news of my father's sudden death. I was quite calm and he seemed surprised, but the truth was that I hadn't taken it in, I didn't believe him.

Harrogate was full of music that late summer. Concertinas, harpists, barrel organs, singers. One afternoon in an unfamiliar street, listening to a man singing 'It may be for years and it may be for ever', I burst into tears and once started I couldn't stop.

Soon I was packed off to responsible Aunt Clare in Wales. 'You cry without reticence,' she told me the day after I arrived. 'And you watch me without reticence,' I thought.

There was a calm slow-moving river called the Afon that flowed at the bottom of my aunt's garden. Walking up and down looking at the water she said that she could understand my grief. My father's death meant that it was impossible to keep me in London at a theatrical school. 'Quite out of the question.' She had heard from my mother who wished me to return home at once. I said that I didn't want to go, 'not yet'. 'But you'll have to.' 'I won't....'

Aunt Clare changed the subject. 'What a lovely day. Straight from the lap of the gods' (she talked like that). As her voice went on I was repeating to myself 'Straight from the lap of the gods'.

At last we went up to London to do some shopping for hot weather clothes and one afternoon when she was visiting friends I went to Blackmore's agency in the Strand and after some palaver was engaged as one of the chorus of a touring musical comedy. I was astonished when Aunt Clare told me that I'd behaved deceitfully, outrageously. A heated argument followed.

She said that my contract had no legal value at my age and threatened to stop me. I said that if she stopped me I'd marry a young man at the Academy whom I knew she detested. He'd been to tea at the Marylebone flat. 'He may be a horrid boy but he's got a lot of money.' 'How do you know that?' said my aunt in a different voice, a sharp voice.

'He showed me the letter from his trustees. He's twenty-one. Besides at the Academy everyone knows who has money and who hasn't. That's one thing they do know.'

'If this young man is well-off you ought to think very carefully before you answer him.'

'I have answered him. I said no. But if you interfere with my contract I'll marry him and be miserable. And it will be your fault.'

This went on for a long time. Then Aunt Clare said that it was unfair to expect her to deal with me, that she'd write to my mother. 'Perhaps we'll be rehearsing before she answers,' I said hopefully. But when my mother's letter arrived it was very vague. She didn't approve, neither did she altogether disapprove. It seemed as if what with her grief for my father and her worry about money she was relieved that I'd be earning my own living in England. 'Not much of a living,' said my aunt.

'Some people manage. Why shouldn't I?'

The company was playing a musical comedy called *Our Miss Gibbs*. We rehearsed at the National Sporting Club somewhere in the Leicester Square/Covent Garden area. A large room with a stage up one end. Sometimes boxers would pass through looking rather shy on their way to other rooms, I

supposed. It was foggy. First a black fog then a yellow one. I
didn't feel well but I never missed a rehearsal. Once my aunt
came with me and the girls approved of her so enthusiastically
that I saw her in a new light. 'Is that your auntie? Oh, isn't she
nice.'

She was a nice woman, I see that now. It was kind of her to
take charge of me to please her favourite brother. But she
wasn't exactly demonstrative. Even pecks on the cheek were
very rare. And I craved for affection and reassurance. By far
my nicest Cambridge memory was of the day an undergradu-
ate on a bicycle knocked me flat as I was crossing the road. I
wasn't hurt but he picked me up so carefully and apologized so
profusely that I thought about him for a long time.

Talking to the other girls I realized that several of them
dreaded the tour up North in the winter. We were going to
Oldham, Bury, Leeds, Halifax, Huddersfield and so on. As for
the boys, one of them showed me a sketch he'd done of a street
in a northern town. He'd called it 'Why we drink'. But none of
this prevented me from being excited and happy.

The man who engaged me at the agent's was at one
rehearsal. He came up to me and said in a low voice: 'Don't tell
the other girls that you were at Tree's School. They mightn't
like it.' I hadn't any idea what he meant. But 'No, I won't tell
anybody,' I promised.

On Not Shooting Sitting Birds

There is no control over memory. Quite soon you find yourself being vague about an event which seemed so important at the time that you thought you'd never forget it. Or unable to recall the face of someone whom you could have sworn was there for ever. On the other hand, trivial and meaningless memories may stay with you for life. I can still shut my eyes and see Victoria grinding coffee on the pantry steps, the glass bookcase and the books in it, my father's pipe-rack, the leaves of the sandbox tree, the wallpaper of the bedroom in some shabby hotel, the hairdresser in Antibes. It's in this way that I remember buying the pink Milanese silk under-clothes, the assistant who sold them to me and coming into the street holding the parcel.

I had started out in life trusting everyone and now I trusted no one. So I had few acquaintances and no close friends. It was perhaps in reaction against the inevitable loneliness of my life that I'd find myself doing bold, risky, even outrageous things without hesitation or surprise. I was usually disappointed in these adventures and they didn't have much effect on me, good or bad, but I never quite lost the hope of something better or different.

One day, I've forgotten now where, I met this young man who smiled at me and when we had talked a bit I agreed to have dinner with him in a couple of days' time. I went home excited, for I'd liked him very much, and began to plan what I should wear. I had a dress I quite liked, an evening cloak, shoes, stockings, but my underclothes weren't good enough for the occasion, I decided. Next day I went out and bought the Milanese silk chemise and drawers.

So there we were seated at a table having dinner with a bedroom very obvious in the background. He was younger than I'd thought and stiffer and I didn't like him much after all. He kept eyeing me in such a wary, puzzled way. When we had finished our soup and the waiter had taken the plates away, he said: 'But you're a lady, aren't you?' exactly as he might have said, 'But you're really a snake or a crocodile, aren't you?'

'Oh no, not that you'd notice,' I said, but this didn't work. We looked glumly at each other across the gulf that had yawned between us.

Before I came to England I'd read many English novels and I imagined I knew all about the thoughts and tastes of various sorts of English people. I quickly decided that to distract or interest this man I must talk about shooting.

I asked him if he knew the West Indies at all. He said no, he didn't and I told him a long story of having been lost in the Dominican forest when I was a child. This wasn't true. I'd often been in the woods but never alone. 'There are no parrots now,' I said, 'or very few. There used to be. There's a Dominican parrot in the zoo – have you ever seen it? – a sulky bird, very old I think. However, there are plenty of other birds and we do have shooting parties. Perdrix are very good to eat, but ramiers are rather bitter.'

Then I began describing a fictitious West Indian shooting party and all the time I talked I was remembering the real thing. An old shotgun leaning up in one corner of the room, the round table in the middle where we would sit to make cartridges, putting the shot in, ramming it down with a wad of paper. Gunpowder? There was that too, for I remember the smell. I suppose the boys were trusted to be careful.

The genuine shooting party consisted of my two brothers, who shared the shotgun, some hangers-on and me at the end of the procession, for then I couldn't bear to be left out of anything. As soon as the shooting was about to start I would stroll away casually and when I was out of sight run as hard as I could, crouch down behind a bush and put my fingers in my ears. It wasn't that I was sorry for the birds, but I hated and feared the noise of the gun. When it was all over I'd quietly join the others. I must have done this unobtrusively or probably my brothers thought me too insignificant to worry about, for no one ever remarked on my odd behaviour or teased me about it.

On and on I went, almost believing what I was saying, when he interrupted me. 'Do you mean to say that your brothers shot sitting birds?' His voice was cold and shocked.

I stared at him. How could I convince this man that I hadn't the faintest idea whether my brothers shot sitting birds or not? How could I explain now what really happened? If I did he'd think me a liar. Also a coward and there he'd be right, for I was afraid of many things, not only the sound of gunfire. But by this time I wasn't sure that I liked him at all so I was silent and felt my face growing as stiff and unsmiling as his.

It was a most uncomfortable dinner. We both avoided looking at the bedroom and when the last mouthful was swallowed he announced that he was going to take me home. The way he said this rather puzzled me. Then I told myself that probably he was curious to see where I lived. Neither of us spoke in the taxi except to say, 'Well, goodnight.' 'Goodnight.'

I felt regretful when it came to taking off my lovely pink chemise, but I could still think: Some other night perhaps, another sort of man.

I slept at once.

The Insect World

Audrey began to read. Her book was called *Nothing So Blue*. It was set in the tropics. She started at the paragraph which described the habits of an insect called the jigger.

Almost any book was better than life, Audrey thought. Or rather, life as she was living it. Of course, life would soon change, open out, become quite different. You couldn't go on if you didn't hope that, could you? But for the time being there was no doubt that it was pleasant to get away from it. And books could take her away.

She could give herself up to the written word as naturally as a good dancer to music or a fine swimmer to water. The only difficulty was that after finishing the last sentence she was left with a feeling at once hollow and uncomfortably full. Exactly like indigestion. It was perhaps for this reason that she never forgot that books were one thing and that life was another.

When it came to life Audrey was practical. She accepted all she was told to accept. And there had been quite a lot of it. She had been in London for the last five years but for one short holiday. There had been the big blitz, then the uneasy lull, then the little blitz, now the fly bombs. But she still accepted all she was told to accept, tried to remember all she was told to remember. The trouble was that she could not always forget all she was told to forget. She could not forget, for instance, that on her next birthday she would be twenty-nine years of age. Not a Girl any longer. Not really. The war had already gobbled up several years and who knew how long it would go on. Audrey dreaded growing old. She disliked and avoided old people and thought with horror of herself as old. She had never told anyone her real and especial reason for loathing the war. She had never spoken of it – even to her friend Monica.

Monica, who was an optimist five years younger than Audrey, was sure that the war would end soon.

'People always think that wars will end soon. But they don't,' said Audrey. 'Why, one lasted for a hundred years. What about that?

Monica said: 'But that was centuries ago and quite different. Nothing to do with Now.'

But Audrey wasn't at all sure that it was so very different.

'It's as if I'm twins,' she had said to Monica one day in an attempt to explain herself. 'Do you ever feel like that?' But it seemed that Monica never did feel like that or if she did she didn't want to talk about it.

Yet there it was. Only one of the twins accepted. The other felt lost, betrayed, forsaken, a wanderer in a very dark wood. The other told her that all she accepted so meekly was quite mad, potty. And here even books let her down, for no book – at least no book that Audrey had ever read – even hinted at this essential wrongness or pottiness.

Only yesterday, for instance, she had come across it in *Nothing So Blue*. *Nothing So Blue* belonged to her, for she often bought books – most of them Penguins, but some from second-hand shops. She always wrote her name on the fly-leaf and tried to blot out any signs of previous ownership. But this book had been very difficult. It had taken her more than an hour to rub out the pencil marks that had been found all through it. They began harmlessly, 'Read and enjoyed by Charles Edwin Roofe in this Year of our Salvation MCMXLII, which being interpreted is Thank You Very Much', continued 'Blue? Rather pink, I think', and, throughout the whole of the book, the word 'blue' – which of course often occurred – was underlined and in the margin there would be a question mark, a note of exclamation, or 'Ha, ha'. 'Nauseating', he had written on the page which began 'I looked her over and decided she would do'. Then came the real love affair with the beautiful English girl who smelt of daffodils and Mr Roofe had relapsed into 'Ha, ha – sez you!' But it was on page 166 that Audrey had a shock. He had written 'Women are an unspeakable abomination' with such force that the pencil had driven through the paper. She had torn the page out and thrown it into the fireplace. Fancy that! There was no fire, of course, so she was able to pick it up, smooth it out and stick it back.

'Why should I spoil my book?' she had thought. All the same she felt terribly down for some reason. And yet, she told herself, 'I bet if you met that man he would be awfully ordinary, just like everybody else.' It was something about his small, neat precise handwriting that made her think so. But it was always the most ordinary things that suddenly turned round and showed you another face, a terrifying face. That was the hidden horror, the horror everybody pretended did not exist, the horror that was responsible for all the other horrors.

The book was not so cheering, either. It was about damp, moist heat, birds that did not sing, flowers that had no scent. Then there was this horrible girl whom the hero simply had to make love to, though he didn't really want to, and when the lovely, cool English girl heard about it she turned him down.

The natives were surly. They always seemed to be jeering behind your back. And they were stupid. They believed everything they were told, so that they could be easily worked up against somebody. Then they became cruel – so horribly cruel, you wouldn't believe....

And the insects. Not only the rats, snakes and poisonous spiders, scorpions, centipedes, millions of termites in their earth-coloured nests from which branched out yards of elaborately built communication lines leading sometimes to a smaller nest, sometimes to an untouched part of the tree on which they were feeding, while sometimes they just petered out, empty. It was no use poking at a nest with a stick. It seemed vulnerable, but the insects would swarm, whitely horrible, to its defence, and would rebuild it in a night. The only thing was to smoke them out. Burn them alive-oh. And even then some would escape and at once start building somewhere else.

Finally, there were the minute crawling unseen things that got at you as you walked along harmlessly. Most horrible of all these was the jigger.

Audrey stopped reading. She had a headache. Perhaps that was because she had not had anything to eat all day; unless you can count a cup of tea at eight in the morning as something to eat. But she did not often get a weekday off and when she did not a moment must be wasted. So from ten to two, regardless of sirens wailing, she went shopping in Oxford Street, and she skipped lunch. She bought stockings, a nightgown and a dress. It was buying the dress that had taken it out of her. The assistant had tried to sell her a print dress a size too big and, when she did not want it, had implied that it was unpatriotic to make so much fuss about what she wore. 'But the colours are so glaring and it doesn't fit. It's much too short,' Audrey said.

'You could easily let it down.'

Audrey said: 'But there's nothing to let down. I'd like to try on that dress over there.'

'It's a very small size.'

'Well, I'm thin enough,' said Audrey defiantly. 'How much thinner d'you want me to be?'

'But that's a dress for a girl,' the assistant said.

And suddenly, what with the pain in her back and everything, Audrey had wanted to cry. She nearly said 'I work just as hard as you,' but she was too dignified.

'The grey one looks a pretty shape,' she said. 'Not so drear. Drear,' she repeated, because that was a good word and if the assistant knew anything she would place her by it. But the woman, not at all impressed, stared over her head.

'The dresses on that rail aren't your size. You can try one on if you like but it wouldn't be any use. You could easily let down the print one,' she repeated maddeningly.

Audrey had felt like a wet rag after her defeat by the shop assistant, for she had ended by buying the print dress. It would not be enough to go and spruce up in the Ladies' Room on the fifth floor – which would be milling full of Old Things – so she had gone home again, back to the flat she shared with Monica. There had not been time to eat anything, but she had put on the new dress and it looked even worse than it had looked in the shop. From the neck to the waist it was enormous, or shapeless. The skirt, on the other hand, was very short and skimpy and two buttons came off in her hand; she had to wait and sew them on again.

It had all made her very tired. And she would be late for tea at Roberta's....

'I wish I lived here,' she thought when she came out of the Tube station. But she often thought that when she went to a different part of London. 'It's nicer here,' she'd think, 'I might be happier here.'

Her friend Roberta's house was painted green and had a small garden. Audrey felt envious as she pressed the bell. And still more envious when Roberta came to the door wearing a flowered house coat, led the way into a pretty sitting-room and collapsed onto her sofa in a film-star attitude. Audrey's immediate thought was 'What right has a woman got to be lolling about like that in wartime, even if she is going to have a baby?' But when she noticed Roberta's deep-circled eyes, her huge, pathetic stomach, her spoilt hands, her broken nails, and realized that her house coat had been made out of a pair of old curtains ('not half so pretty as she was. Looks much older') she said the usual things, warmly and sincerely.

But she hoped that, although it was nearly six by the silver clock, Roberta would offer her some tea and cake. Even a plain slice of bread – she could have wolfed that down.

'Why are you so late?' Roberta asked. 'I suppose you've had tea,' and hurried on before Audrey could open her mouth. 'Have a chocolate biscuit.'

So Audrey ate a biscuit slowly. She felt she did not know Roberta well enough to say 'I'm ravenous. I must have something to eat.' Besides that was the funny thing. The more ravenous you grew, the more impossible it became to say 'I'm ravenous!'

'Is that a good book?' Roberta asked.

'I brought it to read on the Tube. It isn't bad.'

Roberta flicked through the pages of *Nothing So Blue* without much interest. And she said 'English people always mix up tropical places. My dear, I met a girl the other day who thought Moscow was the capital of India! Really, I think it's dangerous to be as ignorant as that, don't you?'

Roberta often talked about 'English' people in that way. She had acquired the habit, Audrey thought, when she was out of England for two years before the war. She had lived for six months in New York. Then she had been to Miami, Trinidad, Bermuda – all those places – and no expense spared, or so she said. She had brought back all sorts of big ideas. Much too big. Gadgets for the kitchen. An extensive wardrobe. Expensive makeup. Having her hair and nails looked after every week at the hairdresser's. There was no end to it. Anyway, there was one good thing about the war. It had taken all that right off.

Right off.

'Read what he says about jiggers,' Audrey said.

'My dear,' said Roberta, 'he *is* piling it on.'

'Do you mean that there aren't such things as jiggers?'

'Of course there are such things,' Roberta said, 'but they're only sand fleas. It's better not to go barefoot if you're frightened of them.'

She explained about jiggers. They had nasty ways – the man wasn't so far wrong. She talked about tropical insects for some time after that; she seemed to remember them more vividly than anything else. Then she read out bits of *Nothing So Blue*, laughing at it.

'If you must read all the time, you needn't believe everything you read.'

'I don't,' said Audrey. 'If you knew how little I really believe you'd be surprised. Perhaps he doesn't see it the way you do. It all depends on how people see things. If someone wanted to write a horrible book about London, couldn't he write a horrible book? I wish somebody would. I'd buy it.'

'You dope!' said Roberta affectionately.

When the time came to go Audrey walked back to the Tube station in a daze, and in a daze sat in the train until a jerk of the brain warned her that she had passed Leicester Square and now had to change at King's Cross. She felt very bad when she got out, as if she could flop any minute. There were so many people pushing, you got bewildered.

She tried to think about Monica, about the end of the journey, above all about food – warm, lovely food – but something had happened inside her head and she couldn't concentrate. She kept remembering the termites. Termites running along one of the covered ways that peter out and lead to nothing. When she came to the escalator she hesitated, afraid to get on it. The people clinging to the sides looked very like large insects. No, they didn't *look* like large insects: they were insects.

She got onto the escalator and stood staidly on the right-hand side. No running up for her tonight. She pressed her arm against her side and felt the book. That started her thinking about jiggers again. Jiggers got in under your skin when you didn't know it and laid eggs inside you. Just walking along, as you might be walking along the street to a Tube station, you caught a jigger as easily as you bought a newspaper or turned on the radio. And there you were – infected – and not knowing a thing about it.

In front of her stood an elderly woman with dank hair and mean-looking clothes. It was funny how she hated women like that. It was funny how she hated most women anyway. Elderly women ought to stay at home. They oughtn't to walk about. Depressing people! Jutting out, that was what the woman was doing. Standing right in the middle, instead of in line. So that you could hardly blame the service girl, galloping up in a hurry, for giving her a good shove and saying under her breath 'Oh get out of the way!' But she must have shoved too hard for the old thing tottered. She was going to fall. Audrey's heart jumped sickeningly into her mouth as she shut her eyes. She didn't want to see what it would look like, didn't want to hear the scream.

But no scream came and when Audrey opened her eyes she saw that the old woman had astonishingly saved herself. She had only stumbled down a couple of steps and clutched the rail again. She even managed to laugh and say 'Now I know where all the beef goes to!' Her face, though, was very white. So was Audrey's. Perhaps her heart kept turning over. So did Audrey's.

Even when she got out of the Tube the nightmare was not over. On the way home she had to walk up a little street which she hated and it was getting dark now. It was one of those streets which are nearly always empty. It had been badly blitzed and Audrey was sure that it was haunted. Weeds and wild-looking flowers were growing over the skeleton houses, over the piles of rubble. There were front doorsteps which looked as though they were hanging by a thread, and near one of them lived a black cat with green eyes. She liked cats but not this one, not this one. She was sure it wasn't a cat really.

Supposing the siren went? 'If the siren goes when I'm in this street it'll mean that it's all U.P. with me.' Supposing a man with a strange blank face and no eyebrows – like that one who got into the Ladies at the cinema the other night and stood there grinning at them and nobody knew what to do so everybody pretended he wasn't there. Perhaps he was *not* there, either – supposing a man like that were to come up softly behind her, touch her shoulder, speak to her, she wouldn't be able to struggle, she would just lie down and die of fright, so much she hated that street. And she had to walk slowly because if she ran she would give whatever it was its opportunity and it would run after her. However, even walking slowly, it came to an end at last. Just round the corner in a placid ordinary street where all the damage had been tidied up was the third floor flat which she shared with Monica, also a typist in a government office.

The radio was on full tilt. The smell of cabbage drifted down the stairs. Monica, for once, was getting the meal ready. They ate out on Mondays, Wednesdays and Fridays, in on Tuesdays, Thursdays, Saturdays and Sundays. Audrey usually did the housework and cooking and Monica took charge of the ration books, stood in long queues to shop and lugged the laundry back and forwards every week because the van didn't call any longer.

'Hullo,' said Monica.

Audrey answered her feebly, 'Hullo.'

Monica, a dark, pretty girl, put the food on the table and remarked at once, 'You're a bit green in the face. Have you been drinking mock gin?'

'Oh, don't be funny. I haven't had much to eat today – that's all.'

After a few minutes Monica said impatiently, 'Well why don't you eat then?'

'I think I've gone past it,' said Audrey, fidgeting with the sausage and cabbage on her plate.

Monica began to read from the morning paper. She spoke loudly above the music on the radio.

'Have you seen this article about being a woman in Germany? It says they can't get any scent or eau-de-cologne or nail polish.'

'Fancy that!' Audrey said. 'Poor things!'

'It says the first thing Hitler stopped was nail polish. He began that way. I wonder why. He must have had a reason, mustn't he?'

'Why must he have had a reason?' said Audrey.

'Because,' said Monica, 'if they've got a girl thinking she

isn't pretty, thinking she's shabby, they've got her where they want her, as a rule. And it might start with nail polish, see? And it says: "All the old women and the middle-aged women look most terribly unhappy. They simply *slink* about," it says.'

'You surprise me,' Audrey said. 'Different in the Isle of Dogs, isn't it?'

She was fed up now and she wanted to be rude to somebody. 'Oh *do* shut up,' she said. 'I'm not interested. Why should I have to cope with German women as well as all the women over here? What a nightmare!'

Monica opened her mouth to answer sharply; then shut it again. She was an even-tempered girl. She piled the plates onto a tray, took it into the kitchen and began to wash up.

As soon as she had gone. Audrey turned off the radio and the light. Blissful sleep, lovely sleep, she never got enough of it.... On Sunday mornings, long after Monica was up, she would lie unconscious. A heavy sleeper, you might call her, expect that her breathing, was noiseless and shallow and that she lay so still, without tossing or turning. And then *She (who?) sent the gentle sleep from Heaven that slid into my soul. That slid into my soul. Sleep, Nature's sweet, something-or-the-other. The sleep that knits up the ravelled....*

It seemed that she had hardly shut her eyes when she was awake again. Monica was shaking her.

'What's the matter? Is it morning?' Audrey said. 'What is it? What is it?'

'Oh, nothing at all,' Monica said sarcastically. 'You were only shrieking the place down.'

'Was I?' Audrey said, interested. 'What was I saying?'

'I don't know what you were saying and I don't care. But if you're trying to get us turned out, that's the way to do it. You know perfectly well that the woman downstairs is doing all she can to get us out because she says we are too noisy. You said something about jiggers. What *are* jiggers anyway?'

'It's slang for people in the Tube.' Audrey answered glibly to her great surprise. 'Didn't you know that?'

'Oh is it? No, I never heard that.'

'The name comes from a tropical insect,' Audrey said, 'that gets in under your skin when you don't know it. It lays eggs and hatches them out and you don't know it. And there's another sort of tropical insect that lives in enormous cities. They have railways, Tubes, bridges, soldiers, wars, everything we have. And they have big cities, and smaller cities with roads going from one to another. Most of them are what they call workers. They never fly because they've lost their wings and they never make love either. They're just workers. Nobody quite knows how this is done, but they think it's the food. Other people say it's segregation. Don't you believe me?' she said, her voice rising. 'Do you think I'm telling lies?'

'Of course I believe you,' said Monica soothingly, 'but I don't see why you should shout about it.'

Audrey drew a deep breath. The corners of her mouth quivered. Then she said 'Look I'm going to bed. I'm awfully tired. I'm going to take six aspirins and then go to bed. If the siren goes don't wake me up. Even if one of those things seems to be coming very close, don't wake me up. I don't want to be woken up whatever happens.'

'Very well,' Monica said. 'All right, old girl.'

Audrey rushed at her with clenched fists and began to shriek again. 'Damn you, don't call me that. Damn your soul to everlasting hell *don't call me that*....'

Till September Petronella

There was a barrel organ playing at the corner of Torrington Square. It played *Destiny* and *La Paloma* and *Le Rêve Passe*, all tunes I liked, and the wind was warm and kind not spiteful, which doesn't often happen in London. I packed the striped dress that Estelle had helped me to choose, and the cheap white one that fitted well, and my best underclothes, feeling very happy while I was packing. A bit of a change, for that had not been one of my lucky summers.

I would tell myself it was the colour of the carpet or something about my room which was depressing me, but it wasn't that. And it wasn't anything to do with money either. I was making nearly five pounds a week – very good for me, and different from when I first started, when I was walking round trying to get work. *No* Hawkers, *No* Models, some of them put up, and you stand there, your hands cold and clammy, afraid to ring the bell. But I had got past that stage; this depression had nothing to do with money.

I often wished I was like Estelle, this French girl who lived in the big room on the ground floor. She had everything so cut-and-dried, she walked the tightrope so beautifully, not even knowing she was walking it. I'd think about the talks we had, and her clothes and her scent and the way she did her hair, and that when I went into her room it didn't seem like a Bloomsbury bed-sitting room – and when it comes to Bloomsbury bed-sitting rooms I know what I'm talking about. No, it was like a room out of one of those long, romantic novels, six hundred and fifty pages of small print, translated from French or German or Hungarian or something – because few of the English ones have the exact feeling I mean. And you read one page of it or even one phrase of it, and then you gobble up all the rest and go about in a dream for weeks afterwards, for months afterwards – perhaps all your life, who knows? – surrounded by those six hundred and fifty pages, the houses, the streets, the snow, the river, the roses, the girls, the sun, the ladies' dresses and the gentlemen's voices, the old, wicked, hard-hearted women and the old, sad women, the waltz music, everything. What is not there you put in afterwards, for it is alive, this book, and it grows in your head. 'The house I was living in when I read this book,' you think, or 'This colour reminds me of that book.'

It was after Estelle left, telling me she was going to Paris and wasn't sure whether she was coming back, that I struck a bad patch. Several of the people I was sitting to left London in June, but, instead of arranging for more work, I took long walks, zigzag, always the same way – Euston Road, Hampstead Road, Camden Town – though I hated those streets, which were like a grey nightmare in the sun. You saw so many old women, or women who seemed old, peering at the vegetables in the Camden Town market, looking at you with hatred, or blankly, as though they had forgotten your language, and talked another one. 'My God,' I would think, 'I hope I never live to be old. Anyway, however old I get, I'll never let my hair go grey. I'll dye it black, red, any colour you like, but I'll never let it go grey. I hate grey too much.' Coming back from one of these walks the thought came to me suddenly, like a revelation, that I could kill myself any time I liked and so end it. After that I put a better face on things.

When Marston wrote and I told the landlord I was going away for a fortnight, he said 'So there's a good time coming for the ladies, is there? – a good time coming for the girls? About time too.'

Marston said, 'You seem very perky, my dear. I hardly recognized you.'

I looked along the platform, but Julian had not come to meet me. There was only Marston, his long, white face and his pale-blue eyes, smiling.

'What a gigantic suitcase', he said. 'I have my motorbike here, but I suppose I'd better leave it. We'll take a cab.'

It was getting dark when we reached the cottage, which stood by itself on rising ground. There were two elm trees in a field near the verandah, but the country looked bare, with low, grassy hills.

As we walked up the path through the garden I could hear Julian laughing and a girl talking, her voice very high and excited, though she put on a calm, haughty expression as we came into the room. Her dress was red, and she wore several coloured glass bangles which tinkled when she moved.

Marston said, 'This is Frankie. You've met the great Julian, of course.'

Well, I knew Frankie Morell by sight, but as she didn't say anything about it I didn't either. We smiled at each other cautiously, falsely.

The table was laid for four people. The room looked comfortable but there were no flowers. I had expected that they would have it full of flowers. However, there were some sprays of honeysuckle in a green jug in my bedroom and Marston, standing in the doorway, said, 'I walked miles to get you that honeysuckle this morning. I thought about you all the time I was picking it.'

'Don't be long,' he said. 'We're all very hungry.'

We ate ham and salad and drank perry. It went to my head a bit. Julian talked about his job which he seemed to dislike. He was the music critic of one of the daily papers. 'It's a scandal. One's forced to down the right people and praise the wrong people.'

'Forced?' said Marston.

'Well, they drop very strong hints.'

'I'll take the plates away,' Frankie told me. 'You can start tomorrow. Not one of the local women will do a thing for us. We've only been here a fortnight, but they've got up a hate you wouldn't believe. Julian says he almost faints when he thinks of it. I say, why think of it?'

When she came back she turned the lamp out. Down there it was very still. The two trees outside did not move, or the moon.

Julian lay on the sofa and I was looking at his face and his hair when Marston put his arms round me and kissed me. But I watched Julian and listened to him whistling – stopping, laughing, beginning again.

'What was that music?' I said, and Frankie answered in a patronizing voice, '*Tristan*, second act duet.'

'I've never been to that opera.'

I had never been to any opera. All the same, I could imagine it. I could imagine myself in a box, wearing a moonlight-blue dress and silver shoes, and when the lights went up everybody asking, 'Who's that lovely girl in that box?' But it must happen quickly or it will be too late.

Marston squeezed my hand. 'Very fine performance, Julian,' he said, 'very fine. Now forgive me, my dears, I must leave you. All this emotion –'

Julian lighted the lamp, took a book from the shelf and began to read.

Frankie blew on the nails of one hand and polished them on the edge of the other. Her nails were nice – of course, you could get a manicure for a bob then – but her hands were large and too white for her face. 'I've seen you at the Apple Tree, surely.' The Apple Tree was a night club in Greek Street.

'Oh yes, often.'

'But you've cut your hair. I wanted to cut mine, but Julian asked me not to. He begged me not to. Didn't you, Julian?'

Julian did not answer

'He said he'd lose his strength if I cut my hair.'

Julian turned over a page and went on reading.

'This isn't a bad spot, is it?' Frankie said. 'Not one of those places where the ceiling's on top of your head and you've got to walk four miles in the dark to the lavatory. There are two other bedrooms besides the one Marston gave you. Come and have a look at them. You can change over if you want to. We'll never tear Julian away from his book. It's about the biological inferiority of women. That's what you told me, Julian, isn't it?'

'Oh, *go* away,' Julian said.

We ended up in her room, where she produced some head and figure studies, photographs.

'Do you like these? Do you know this man? He says I'm the best model he's ever had. He says I'm far and away the best model in London.'

'Beautiful. Lovely photographs.'

But Frankie, sitting on the big bed, said, 'Aren't people swine? Julian says I never think. He's wrong, sometimes I think quite a lot. The other day I spent a long time trying to decide which were worse – men or women.'

'I wonder.'

'Women are worse.'

She had long, calm black hair, drawn away from her face and hanging smoothly almost to her waist, and a calm, clear little voice and a calm, haughty expression.

'They'll kick your face to bits if you let them. And shriek with laughter at the damage. But I'm not going to let them – oh no…Marston's always talking about you,' she said. 'He's very fond of you, poor old Marston. Do you know that picture as you go into his studio – in the entrance place? What's he say it is?'

'The Apotheosis of Lust.'

'Yes, the Apotheosis of Lust. I have to laugh when I think of that, for some reason. Poor old Andy Marston…. But I don't know why I should say "Poor old Andy Marston". He'll always have one penny to tinkle against another. His family's wealthy, you know.'

'He makes me go cold.'

I thought, 'Why did I say that?' Because I like Marston.

'So that's how you feel about him, is it?' She seemed pleased, as if she had heard something she wanted to hear, had been waiting to hear.

'Are you tired?' Marston said.

I was looking out of the bedroom window at some sheep feeding in the field where the elm trees grew.

'A bit,' I said. 'A bit very.'

His mouth drooped, disappointed.

'Oh, Marston, thank you for asking me down here. It's so lovely to get away from London; it's like a dream.'

'A dream, my God! However, when it comes to dreams, why shouldn't they be pleasant?'

He sat down on the windowsill.

'The great Julian's not so bad, is he?'

'Why do you call him the great Julian? As if you were gibing at him.'

'Gibing at him? Good Lord, far be it from me to gibe at him. He *is* the great Julian. He's going to be very important, so far as an English musician can be important. He's horribly conceited, though. Not about his music, of course – he's conceited about his personal charm. I can't think why. He's a very ordinary type really. You see that nose and mouth and hear that voice all over the place. You rather dislike him, don't you?'

'Do I?'

'Of course you do. Have you forgotten how annoyed you were when I told you that he'd have to *see* a female before he could consent to live at close quarters with her for two weeks? You were quite spirited about it, I thought. Don't say that was only a flash in the pan, you poor devil of a female, female, female, in a country where females are only tolerated at best! What's going to become of you, Miss Petronella Gray, living in a bed-sitting room in Torrington Square, with no money, no background and no nous?... Is Petronella your real name?'

'Yes.'

'You worry me, whatever your name is. I bet it isn't Gray.'

I thought, 'What does it matter? If you knew how bloody my home was you wouldn't be surprised that I wanted to change my name and forget all about it.'

I said, not looking at him, 'I was called after my grandmother – Julia Petronella.'

'Oh, you've got a grandmother, have you? Fancy that! Now, for Heaven's sake don't put on that expression. Take my advice and grow another skin or two and sharpen your claws before it's too late. *Before it's too late*, mark those words. If you don't, you're going to have a hell of a time.'

'So that I long for death?'

He looked startled. 'Why do you say that?'

'It was only the first thing that came into my head from nowhere. I was joking.'

When he did not answer, 'Well, good night,' I said. 'Sleep tight.'

'I shan't sleep,' he said. 'I shall probably have to listen to those two for quite a time yet. When they're amorous they're noisy and when they fight it's worse. She goes for him with a pen-knife. Mind you, she only does that because he likes it, but her good nature is a pretence. She's a bitch really. Shut your door and you won't hear anything. Will you be sad tomorrow?'

'Of course not.'

'Don't look as if you'd lost a shilling and found sixpence then,' he said, and went out.

That's the way they always talk. 'You look as if you'd lost a shilling and found sixpence,' they say; 'You look very perky, I hardly recognized you,' they say; '*Look gay*,' they say. 'My dear Petronella, I have an entirely new idea of you. I'm going to paint you out in the opulent square. So can you wear something gay tomorrow afternoon? Not one of those drab affairs you usually clothe yourself in. Gay – do you know the meaning of the word? Think about it, it's very important.'

The things you remember....

Once, left alone in a very ornate studio, I went up to a plaster cast – the head of a man, one of those Greek heads – and kissed it, because it was so beautiful. Its mouth felt warm, not cold. It was smiling. When I kissed it the room went dead silent and I was frightened. I told Estelle about this one day. 'Does that sound mad?' She didn't laugh. She said, 'Who hasn't kissed a picture or a photograph and suddenly been frightened?'

The music Julian had been whistling was tormenting me. That, and the blind eyes of the plaster cast, and the way the sun shone on the black iron bedstead in my room in Torrington Square on fine days. The bars of the bedstead grin at me. Sometimes I count the knobs on the chest of drawers three times over. 'One of those drab affairs!...'

I began to talk to Julian in my head. Was it to Julian? 'I'm not like that. I'm not at all like that. They're trying to make me like that, but I'm not like that.'

After a while I took a pencil and paper and wrote, 'I love Julian. Julian, I kissed you once, but you didn't know.'

I folded the paper several times and hid it under some clothes in my suitcase. Then I went to bed and slept at once.

Where our path joined the main road there were some cottages. As Marston and I came back from our walk next morning we passed two women in their gardens, which were full of lupins and poppies. They looked at us sullenly, as though they disliked us. When Marston said 'Good morning', they did not answer.

'Surly, priggish brutes,' he muttered, 'but that's how they are.'

The grass round our cottage was long and trampled in

places. There were no flowers.

'They're back,' Marston said. 'There's the motorbike.'

They came out on to the verandah, very spruce; Frankie in her red frock with her hair tied up in a red and blue handkerchief, Julian wearing a brown coat over a blue shirt and shabby grey trousers like Marston's. Very gay, I thought. (*Gay – do you know the meaning of the word?*)

'What's the matter with you, Marston?' Julian said. 'You look frightful.'

'You do seem a bit upset,' Frankie said. 'What happened? Do tell.'

'Don't tell her anything,' said Marston. 'I'm going to dress up too. Why should I be the only one in this resplendent assembly with a torn shirt and stained bags? Wait till you see what I've got – and I don't mean what you mean.'

'Let's get the food ready,' Frankie said to me.

The kitchen table was covered with things they had brought from Cheltenham, and there were several bottles of white wine cooling in a bucket of water in the corner.

'What have you done to Marston?'

'Nothing. What on earth do you mean?'

Nothing had happened. We were sitting under a tree, looking at a field of corn, and Marston put his head in my lap and then a man came along and yelled at us. I said, 'What do you think we're doing to your corn? Can't we even look at your corn?' But Marston only mumbled, 'I'm fearfully sorry. I'm dreadfully sorry,' and so on. And then we went walking along the main road in the sun, not talking much because I was hating him.

'Nothing happened,' I said.

'Oh well, it's a pity, because Julian's in a bad mood today. However, don't take any notice of him. Don't start a row whatever you do; just smooth it over.'

'Look at the lovely bit of steak I got,' she said. 'Marston says he can't touch any meat except cold ham, I ask you, and he does the cooking. Cold ham and risotto, risotto and cold ham. And curried eggs. That's what we've been living on ever since we came down here.'

When we went in with the food they had finished a bottle of

wine. Julian said, 'Here's luck to the ruddy citizens I saw this morning. May they be flourishing and producing offspring exactly like themselves, but far, far worse, long after we are all in our dishonoured graves.'

Marston was now wearing black silk pyjamas with a pattern of red and green dragons. His long, thin neck and sad face looked extraordinary above this get-up. Frankie and I glanced at each other and giggled. Julian scowled at me.

Marston went over to the mirror. 'Never mind,' he said softly to his reflection, 'never mind, never mind.'

'It's ham and salad again,' Frankie said. 'But I've got some prunes.'

The table was near the window. A hot, white glare shone in our eyes. We tried pulling the blinds down, but one got stuck and we went on eating in the glare.

Then Frankie talked about the steak again. 'You must have your first bite tonight, Marston.'

'It won't be my first bite,' Marston said. 'I've been persuaded to taste beef before.'

'Oh, you never told me that. No likee?'

'I thought it would taste like sweat,' Marston said, 'and it did.'

Frankie looked annoyed. 'The trouble with you people is that you try to put other people off just because you don't fancy a thing. If you'd just not like it and leave it at that, but you don't *rest* till you've put everybody else off.'

'Oh God, let's get tight,' Julian said. 'There are bottles and bottles of wine in the kitchen. Cooling, I hope.'

'We'll get them,' Frankie said, 'we'll get them.'

Frankie sat on the kitchen table. 'I think Julian's spoiling for a fight. Let him calm down a bit…. You're staving Marston off, aren't you? And he doesn't like it; he's very disconsolate. You've got to be careful of these people, they can be as hard as nails.'

Far away a dog barked, a cock crew, somebody was sawing wood. I hardly noticed what she had said because again it came, that feeling of happiness, the fish-in-water feeling, so that I couldn't even remember having been unhappy.

Frankie started on a long story about a man called Petersen

who had written a play about Northern gods and goddesses
and Yggdrasil.

'I though Yggdrasil was a girl, but it seems it's a tree.'

Marston and Julian and all that lot had taken Petersen up,
she said. They used to ask him out and make him drunk. Then
he would take his clothes off and dance about and if he did not
do it somebody would be sure to say, 'What's the matter? Why
don't you perform?' But as soon as he got really sordid they
had dropped him like a hot brick. He simply disappeared.

'I met an old boy who knew him and asked what had
happened. The old boy said, "A gigantic maw has swallowed
Petersen...." Maw, what a word! It reminds me of Julian's
mother – she's a maw if you like. Well, I'd better take these
bottles along now.'

So we took the four bottles out of the bucket and went back
into the sitting-room. It was still hot and glaring, but not quite
so bad as it had been.

'Now it's my turn to make a speech,' said Marston. 'But you
must drink, pretty creatures, drink.' He filled our glasses and I
drank mine quickly. He filled it up again.

'My speech,' he said, 'my speech.... Let's drink to afternoon, the best of all times. Cruel morning is past, fearful,
unpredictable, lonely night is yet to come. Here's to heart-
rending afternoon.... I will now recite a poem. It's hackneyed
and pawed about, like so many other things, but beautiful.
"C'est bien la pire peine de ne savoir pourquoi –"'

He stopped and began to cry. We all looked at him. Nobody
laughed; nobody knew what to say. I felt shut in by the glare.

Marston blew his nose, wiped his eyes and gabbled on:
'"Pourquoi, sans amour et sans haine, Mon coeur a tant de peine...."'

'"Sans amour" is right,' Julian said, staring at me. I looked
back into his eyes.

'"But for loving, why, you would not, Sweet,"' Marston
went on, '"Though we prayed you, Paid you, brayed you In a
mortar – for you could not, Sweet."'

'The motorbike was altogether a bit of luck,' Frankie said.
'Julian had a fight with a man on the bus going in. I thought
he'd have a fit.'

'Fight?' Julian said. 'I never fight. I'm frightened.'

He was still staring at me.

'Well then, you were very rude.'

'I'm never rude, either,' Julian said. 'I'm far too frightened ever to be rude. I suffer in silence.'

'I shouldn't do that if I were you,' I said. The wine was making me giddy. So was the glare, and the way he was looking at me.

'What's this young creature up to?' he said. 'I can't quite make her out.'

'Ruddy respectable citizens never can.'

'Ha-hah,' Frankie said. 'One in the eye for you, Julian. You're always going on about respectable people, but you know *you* are respectable, whatever you say and whatever you do and you'll be respectable till you die, however you die, and that way you miss something, believe it or not.'

'You keep out of this, Phoenician,' Julian said. 'You've got nothing to say. Retire under the table, because that's where I like you best.'

Frankie crawled under the table. She darted her head out now and again, pretending to bite his legs, and every time she did that he would shiver and scream.

'Oh, come on out,' he said at last. 'It's too hot for these antics.'

Frankie crawled out again, very pleased with herself, went to the mirror and arranged the handkerchief round her hair. 'Am I really like a Phoenician?'

'Of course you are. A Phoenician from Cornwall, England. Direct descent, I should say.'

'And what's she?' Frankie said. Her eyes looked quite different, like snake's eyes. We all looked quite different – it's funny what drink does.

'That's very obvious too,' Julian said.

'All right, why don't you come straight out with it?' I said. 'Or are you frightened?'

'Sometimes words fail.'

Marston waved his arms about. 'Julian, you stop this. I won't have it.'

'You fool,' Julian said, 'you fool. Can't you see she's fifth-rate. Can't you see?'

'You ghastly cross between a barmaid and a chorus-girl,' he

said; 'You female spider,' he said; You've been laughing at him for weeks,' he said, 'jeering at him, sniggering at him. Stopping him from working – the best painter in this damnable island, the only one in my opinion. And then when I try to get him away from you, of course you follow him down here.'

'That's not it at all,' Marston said. 'You're not being fair to the girl. You don't understand her a bit.'

'She doesn't care,' Julian said. 'Look at her – she's giggling her stupid head off.'

'Well, what are you to do when you come up against a mutual admiration society?' I said.

'You're letting your jealousy run away with you,' said Marston.

'Jealousy?' Julian said. 'Jealousy!' He was unrecognizable. His beautiful eyes were little, mean pits and you looked down them into nothingness.

'Jealous of what?' he shrieked. 'Why, do you know that she told Frankie last night that she can't bear you and that the only reason she has anything to do with you is because she wants money. What do you think of that? Does that open your eyes?'

'Now, *Julian!*' Frankie's voice was as loud and high as his. 'You'd no right to repeat that. You promised you wouldn't and anyway you've exaggerated it. It's all very well for you to talk about how inferior women are, but you get more like your horrible mother every moment.'

'You do,' Marston said, quite calm now. 'Julian, you really do.'

'Do you know what all this is about?' Frankie said, nodding at Julian. 'It's because he doesn't want me to go back to London with him. He wants me to go and be patronized and educated by his detestable mother in her dreary house in the dreary country, who will then say that the case is hopeless. Wasn't she a good sort and a saint to try? But the girl is *quite impossible*. Do you think I don't know that trick? It's as old as the hills.'

'You're mean,' she said to Julian, 'and you hate girls really. Don't imagine I don't see through you. You're trying to get me down. But you won't do it. If you think you're the only man in the world who's fond of me *or* that I'm a goddamned fool, you're making the hell of a big mistake, you and your mother.'

She plucked a hairpin from her hair, bent it into the shape of pince-nez and went on in a mincing voice. 'Do Ay understend you tew say thet *may* sonn –' she placed the pince-nez on her nose and looked over it sourly '– with *one* connection –'

'Damn you,' said Julian, 'damn you, damn you.'

'Now they're off,' Marston said placidly. 'Drinking on a hot afternoon is a mistake. The pen-knife will be out in a minute.... Don't go. Stay and watch the fun. My money on Frankie every time.'

But I went into the bedroom and shut the door. I could hear them wrangling and Marston, very calm and superior, putting in a word now and again. Then nothing. They had gone on to the verandah.

I got the letter I had written and tore it very carefully into four pieces. I spat on each piece. I opened the door – there was not a sign of them. I took the pieces of paper to the lavatory, emptied them in and pulled the plug. As soon as I heard the water gushing I felt better.

The door of the kitchen was open and I saw that there was another path leading to the main road.

And there I was, walking along, not thinking of anything, my eyes fixed on the ground. I walked a long way like that, not looking up, though I passed several people. At last I came to a sign-post. I was on the Cirencester road. Something about the word 'miles' written made me feel very tired.

A little farther on the wall on one side of the road was low. It was the same wall on which Marston and I had sat that morning, and he had said, 'Do you think we could rest here or will the very stones rise up against us?' I looked round and there was nobody in sight, so I stepped over it and sat down in the shade. It was pretty country, but bare. The white, glaring look was still in the sky.

Close by there was a dove cooing. 'Coo away, dove,' I thought. 'It's no use, no use, still coo away, coo away.'

After a while the dazed feeling, as if somebody had hit me on the head, began to go. I though 'Cirencester – and then a train to London. It's as easy as that.'

Then I realized that I had left my handbag and money, as well as everything else, in the bedroom at the cottage, but imagining walking back there made me feel so tired that I could hardly put one foot in front of the other.

I got over the wall. A car that was coming along slowed down and stopped and the man driving it said, 'Want a lift?'

I went up to the car.

'Where do you want to go?'

'I want to go to London.'

'To London? Well, I can't take you as far as that, but I can get you into Cirencester to catch a train if you like.'

I said anxiously, 'Yes – but I must go back first to the place where I've been staying. It's not far.'

'Haven't time for that. I've got an appointment. I'm late already and I mustn't miss it. Tell you what – come along with me. If you'll wait till I've done I can take you to fetch your things.'

I got into the car. As soon as I touched him I felt comforted. Some men are like that.

'Well, you look as if you'd lost a shilling and found sixpence.'

Again I had to laugh.

'That's better. Never does any good to be down in the mouth.'

'We're nearly in Cirencester now,' he said after a while. 'I've got to see a lot of people. This is market day and I'm a farmer. I'll take you to a nice quiet place where you can have a cup of tea while you're waiting.'

He drove to a pub in a narrow street. 'This way in.' I followed him into the bar.

'Good afternoon, Mrs Strickland. Lovely day, isn't it? Will you give my friend a cup of tea while I'm away, and make her comfortable? She's very tired.'

'I will, certainly,' Mrs Strickland said, with a swift glance up and down. 'I expect the young lady would like a nice wash too, wouldn't she?' She was dark and nicely got up, but her voice had a tinny sound.

'Oh, I would.'

I looked down at my crumpled white dress. I touched my face for I knew there must be a red mark where I had lain with it pressed against the ground.

'See you later,' the farmer said.

There were brightly polished taps in the ladies' room and a

very clean red and black tiled floor. I washed my hands, tried to smooth my dress, and powdered my face – Poudre Nildé basanée – but I did it without looking in the glass.

Tea and cakes were laid in a small, dark, stuffy room. There were three pictures of Lady Hamilton, Johnnie Walker advertisements, china bulldogs wearing sailor caps and two calendars. One said January 9th, but the other was right – July 28th, 1914....

'Well, here I am.' He sat heavily down beside me. 'Did Mrs Strickland look after you all right?'

'Very well.'

'Oh, she's a good sort, she's a nice woman. She's known me a long time. Of course, you haven't, have you? But everything's got to have a start.'

Then he said he hadn't done so badly that afternoon and stretched out his legs, looking pleased, looking happy as the day is long.

'What were you thinking about when I came in? You nearly jumped out of your skin.'

'I was thinking about the time.'

'About the time? Oh, don't worry about that. There's plenty of time.'

He produced a large silver case, took out a cigar and lighted it, long and slow. 'Plenty of time,' he said. 'Dark in here, isn't it? So you live in London, do you?'

'Yes.'

'I've often thought I'd like to know a nice girl up in London.'

His eyes were fixed on Lady Hamilton and I knew he was imagining a really lovely girl – all curves, curls, heart and hidden claws. He swallowed, then put his hand over mine.

'I'd like to feel that when I go up to Town there's a friend I could see and have a good time with. You know. And I could give her a good time too. By God, I could. I know what women like.'

'You do?'

'Yes, I do. They like a bit of loving, that's what they like, isn't it? A bit of loving. All women like that. They like it dressed up sometimes – and sometimes not, it all depends. You have to know, and I know. I just know.'

'You've nothing more to learn, have you?'

'Not in that way I haven't. And they like pretty dresses and bottles of scent, and bracelets with blue stones in them. I know. Well, what about it?' he said, but as if he were joking.

I looked away from him at the calendar and did not answer, making my face blank.

'What about it?' he repeated.

'It's nice of you to say you want to see me again – very polite.'

He laughed. 'You think I'm being polite, do you? Well, perhaps – perhaps not. No harm in asking, was there? No offence meant – or taken, I hope. It's all right. I'll take you to get your things and catch your train – and we'll have a bottle of something good before we start off. It won't hurt you. It's bad stuff hurts you, not good stuff. You haven't found that out yet, but you will. Mrs Strickland has some good stuff, I can tell you – good enough for me, and I want the best.'

So we had a bottle of Clicquot in the bar.

He said, 'It puts some life into you, doesn't it?'

It did too. I wasn't feeling tired when we left the pub, nor even sad.

'Well,' he said as we got into the car, 'you've got to tell me where to drive to. And you don't happen to know a little song, do you?'

'That was very pretty,' he said when I stopped. 'You've got a very pretty voice indeed. Give us some more.'

But we were getting near the cottage and I didn't finish the next song because I was nervous and worried that I wouldn't be able to tell him the right turning.

At the foot of the path I thought, 'The champagne worked all right.'

He got out of the car and came with me. When we reached the gate leading into the garden he stood by my side without speaking.

They were on the verandah. We could hear their voices clearly.

'Listen, fool,' Julian was saying, 'listen, half-wit. What I said yesterday has nothing to do with what I say today or what I shall say tomorrow. Why should it?'

'That's what you think,' Frankie said obstinately. 'I don't

agree with you. It might have something to do with it whether you like it or not.'

'Oh, stop arguing, you two,' Marston said. 'It's all very well for you, Julian, but I'm worried about that girl. I'm responsible. She looked so damned miserable. Supposing she's gone and made away with herself. I shall feel awful. Besides, probably I shall be held up to every kind of scorn and obloquy – as usual. And though it's all your fault you'll escape scot-free – also as usual.'

'Are those your friends?' the farmer asked.

'Well, they're my friends in a way…. I have to go in to get my things. It won't take me long.'

Julian said, 'I think, I rather think, Marston, that I hear a female pipe down there. You can lay your fears away. She's not the sort to kill herself. I told you that.'

'Who's that?' the farmer said.

'That's Mr Oakes, one of my hosts.'

'Oh, is it? I don't like the sound of him. I don't like the sound of any of them. Shall I come with you?'

'No, don't. I won't be long.'

I went round by the kitchen into my room, walking very softly. I changed into my dark dress and then began to throw my things into the suitcase. I did all this as quickly as I could, but before I had finished Marston came in, still wearing his black pyjamas crawling with dragons.

'Who were you talking to outside?'

'Oh, that's a man I met. He's going to drive me to Cirencester to catch the London train.'

'You're not offended, are you?'

'Not a bit. Why should I be?'

'Of course, the great Julian can be so difficult,' he murmured. 'But don't think I didn't stick up for you, because I did. I said to him, "It's all very well for you to be rude to a girl I bring down, but what about your loathly Frankie, whom you inflict upon me day after day and week after week and I never say a word? I'm never even sharp to her –" What are you smiling at?'

'The idea of your being sharp to Frankie.'

'The horrid little creature!' Marston said excitedly, 'the unspeakable bitch! But the day will come when Julian will find her out and he'll run to me for sympathy. I'll not give it him.

Not after this…. Cheer up,' he said. 'The world is big. There's hope.'

'Of course.' But suddenly I saw the women's long, scowling faces over their lupins and their poppies, and my room in Torrington Square and the iron bars of my bedstead, and I thought, 'Not for me.'

'It may all be necessary,' he said, as if he were talking to himself. 'One has to get an entirely different set of values to be any good.'

I said, 'Do you think I could go out through the window? I don't want to meet them.'

'I'll come to the car with you. What's this man like?'

'Well, he's a bit like the man this morning, and he says he doesn't care for the sound of you.'

'Then I think I won't come. Go through the window and I'll hand your suitcase to you.'

He leaned out and said, 'See you in September, Petronella. I'll be back in September.'

I looked up at him. 'All right. Same old address.'

The farmer said, 'I was coming in after you. You're well rid of that lot – never did like that sort. Too many of them about.'

'They're all right.'

'Well, tune up,' he said, and I sang 'Mr Brown, Mr Brown, Had a violin, Went around, went around, With his violin.' I sang all the way to Cirencester.

At the station he gave me my ticket and a box of chocolates.

'I bought these for you this afternoon, but I forgot them. Better hurry – there's not much time.'

'Fare you well,' he said. 'That's what they say in Norfolk, where I come from.'

'Good-bye.'

'No, say fare you well.'

'Fare you well.'

The train started.

'This is very nice,' I thought, 'my first-class carriage,' and had a long look at myself in the glass for the first time since it had happened. 'Never mind,' I said, and remembered Marston saying 'Never mind, never mind.'

'Don't look so down in the mouth, my girl,' I said to myself. *'Look gay.'*

'Cheer up,' I said, and kissed myself in the cool glass. I stood with my forehead against it and watched my face clouding gradually, then turned because I felt as if someone was staring at me, but it was only the girl on the cover of the chocolate-box. She had slanting green eyes, but they were too close together, and she had a white, square, smug face that didn't go with her slanting eyes. 'I bet you could be a rotten, respectable, sneering bitch too, with a face like that, if you had the chance,' I told her.

The train got into Paddington just before ten. As soon as I was on the platform I remembered the chocolates, but I didn't go back for them. 'Somebody will find you, somebody will look after you, you rotten, sneering, stupid, tight-mouthed bitch,' I thought.

London always smells the same. 'Frowsty,' you think, 'but I'm glad to be back.' And just for a while it bears you up. 'Anything's round the corner,' you think. But long before you get round the corner it lets you drop.

I decided that I'd walk for a bit with the suitcase and get tired and then perhaps I'd sleep. But at the corner of Marylebone Road and Edgware Road my arm was stiff and I put down the suitcase and waved at a taxi standing by the kerb.

'Sorry, miss,' the driver said, 'this gentleman was first.'

The young man smiled. 'It's all right. You have it.'

'You have it,' he said. The other one said, 'Want a lift?'

'I can get the next one. I'm not in any hurry.'

'Nor am I.'

The taxi-driver moved impatiently.

'Well, don't let's hesitate any longer,' the young man said, 'or we'll lose our taximeter-cab. Get in – I can easily drop you wherever you're going.'

'Go along Edgware Road,' he said to the driver. 'I'll tell you where in a minute.'

The taxi started.

'Where to?'

'Torrington Square.'

The house would be waiting for me. 'When I pass Estelle's

door,' I thought, 'there'll be no smell of scent now.' Then I was back in my small room on the top floor, listening to the church clock chiming every quarter-hour. 'There's a good time coming for the ladies. There's a good time coming for the girls....'

I said, 'Wait a minute. I don't want to go to Torrington Square.'

'Oh, you don't want to go to Torrington Square?' He seemed amused and wary, but more wary than amused.

'It's such a lovely night, so warm. I don't want to go home just yet. I think I'll go and sit in Hyde Park.'

'Not Torrington Square,' he shouted through the window. The taxi drew up.

'Damn his eyes, what's he done that for.'

The driver got down and opened the door.

'Here, where am I going to? This is the third time you've changed your mind since you 'ailed me.'

'You'll go where you're damn well told.'

'Well where am I damn well told?'

'Go to the Marble Arch.'

''Yde Park,' the driver said, looking us up and down and grinning broadly. Then he got back into his seat.

'I can't bear some of these chaps, can you?' the young man said.

When the taxi stopped at the end of Park Lane we both got out without a word. The driver looked us up and down again scornfully before he started away.

'What do you want to do in Hyde Park? Look at the trees?'

He took my suitcase and walked along by my side.

'Yes, I want to look at the trees and not go back to the place where I live. Never go back.'

'I've never lived in a place I like,' I thought, 'never.'

'That does sound desperate. Well, let's see if we can find a secluded spot.'

'That chair over there will do,' I said. It was away from people under a tree. Not that people mattered much, for now it was night and they are never so frightening then.

I shut my eyes so that I could hear and smell the trees better. I imagined I could smell water too. The Serpentine – I didn't know we had walked so far.

He said, 'I can't leave you so disconsolate on this lovely
night – this night of love and night of stars.' He gave a loud
hiccup, and then another. 'That always happens when I've
eaten quails.'

'It happens to me when I'm tight.'

'Does it?' He pulled another chair forward and sat down by
my side. 'I can't leave you now until I know where you're
going with that large suitcase and that desperate expression.'

I told him that I had just come back after a stay in the
country, and he told me that he did not live in London, that his
name was Melville and that he was at a loose end that evening.

'Did somebody let you down?'

'Oh, that's not important – not half so important as the
desperate expression. I noticed that as soon as I saw you.'

'That's not despair, it's hunger,' I said, dropping into the
backchat. 'Don't you know hunger when you see it?'

'Well, let's go and have something to eat, then. But where?'
He looked at me uncertainly. 'Where?'

'We could go to the Apple Tree. Of course, it's a bit early, but
we might be able to get kippers or eggs and bacon or sausages
and mash.'

'The Apple Tree? I've heard of it. Could we go there?' he
said, still eyeing me.

'We could indeed. You could come as my guest. I'm a
member. I was one of the first members,' I boasted.

I had touched the right spring – even the feeling of his hand
on my arm had changed. *Always the same spring to touch before
the sneering expression will go out of their eyes and the sneering
sound out of their voices. Think about it – it's very important.*

'Lots of pretty girls at the Apple Tree, aren't there?' he said.

'I can't promise anything. It's a bad time of year for the
Apple Tree, the singing and the gold.'

'Now what are you talking about?'

'Somebody I know calls it that.'

'But you'll be there.' He pulled his chair closer and looked
round cautiously before he kissed me. 'And you're an awfully
pretty girl, aren't you?...The Apple Tree, the singing and the
gold. I like that.'

'Better than "Night of love and night of stars"?'

'Oh, they're not in the same street.'

I thought, 'How do you know what's in what street? How do they know who's fifth-rate, who's first-rate and where the devouring spider lives?'

'You don't really mind where we go, do you?' he said.

'I don't mind at all.'

He took his arm away. 'It was odd our meeting like that, wasn't it?'

'I don't think so. I don't think it was odd at all.'

After a silence, 'I haven't been very swift in the uptake, have I?' he said.

'No, you haven't. Now, let's be off to the Apple Tree, the singing and the gold.'

'Oh, damn the Apple Tree. I know a better place than that.'

'I've been persuaded to taste it before,' Marston said. 'It tasted exactly as I thought it would.'

And everything was exactly as I had expected. The knowing waiters, the touch of the ice-cold wine glass, the red plush chairs, the food you don't notice, the gold-framed mirror, the bed in the room beyond that always looks as if its ostentatious whiteness hides dinginess....

But Marston should have said, 'It tastes of nothing, my dear, it tastes of nothing....'

When we got out into Leicester Square again I had forgotten Marston and only thought about how, when we had nothing better to do, Estelle and I would go to the Corner House or to some cheap restaurant in Soho and have dinner. She was so earnest when it came to food. 'You must have one good meal a day,' she would say, 'it is *necessary*.' Escalope de veau and fried potatoes and brussels sprouts, we usually had, and then crème caramel or compôte de fruits. And she seemed to be walking along by my side, wearing her blue suit and her white blouse, her high heels tapping. But as we turned the corner by the Hippodrome she vanished. I thought 'I shall never see her again – I know it.'

In the taxi he said, 'I don't forget addresses, do I?'

To keep myself awake I began to sing 'Mr Brown, Mr Brown, Had a violin....'

'Are you on the stage?'

'I was. I started my brilliant and successful career like so many others, in the chorus. But I wasn't a success.'

'What a shame! Why?'

'Because I couldn't say "epigrammatic".'

He laughed – really laughed that time.

'The stage manager had the dotty idea of pulling me out of my obscurity and giving me a line to say. The line was "Oh, Lottie, Lottie, don't be epigrammatic". I rehearsed it and rehearsed it, but when it came to the night it was just a blank.'

At the top of Charing Cross Road the taxi was held up. We were both laughing so much that people turned round and stared at us.

'It was one of the most dreadful moments of my life, and I shan't ever forget it. There was the stage manager, mouthing at me from the wings – he was the prompter too and he also played a small part, the family lawyer – and there he was all dressed up in grey-striped trousers and a black tail-coat and top hat and silver side-whiskers, and there I was, in a yellow dress and a large straw hat and a green sunshade and a lovely background of an English castle and garden – half ruined and half not, you know – and a chorus of footmen and maids, and my mind a complete blank.'

The taxi started again. 'Well, what happened?'

'Nothing. After one second the other actors went smoothly on. I remember the next line. It was "Going to Ascot? Well, if you don't get into the Royal Enclosure when you *are* there I'm no judge of character".'

'But what about the audience?'

'Oh, the audience weren't surprised because, you see, they had never expected me to speak at all. Well, here we are.'

I gave him my latchkey and he opened the door.

'A formidable key! It's like the key of a prison,' he said.

Everyone had gone to bed and there wasn't even a ghost of Estelle's scent in the hall.

'We must see each other again,' he said. 'Please. Couldn't you write to me at –' He stopped. 'No, I'll write to you. If you're ever – I'll write to you anyway.'

I said, 'Do you know what I want? I want a gold bracelet with blue stones in it. Not too blue – the darker blue I prefer.'

'Oh, well.' He was wary again. 'I'll do my best, but I'm not one of these plutocrats, you know.'

'Don't you dare to come back without it. But I'm going away for a few weeks. I'll be here again in September.'

'All right, I'll see you in September, Petronella,' he said chirpily, anxious to be off. 'And you've been so sweet to me.'

'The pleasure was all mine.'

He shook his head. 'Now, Lottie, Lottie, don't be epigrammatic.'

I thought, 'I daresay he would be nice if one got to know him. I daresay, perhaps…' listening to him tapping goodbye on the other side of the door. I tapped back twice and then started up the stairs. Past the door of Estelle's room, not feeling a thing as I passed it, because she had gone and I knew she would not ever come back.

In my room I stood looking out of the window, remembering my yellow dress, the blurred mass of the audience and the face of one man in the front row seen quite clearly, and how I thought, as quick as lightning. 'Help me, tell me what I have forgotten.' But though he had looked, as it seemed, straight into my eyes, and though I was sure he knew exactly what I was thinking, he had not helped me. He had only smiled. He had left me in that moment that seemed like years standing there until through the dreadful blankness of my mind I had heard a high, shrill, cockney voice saying, 'Going to Ascot'? and seen the stage manager frown and shake his head at me.

'My God, I must have looked a fool,' I thought, laughing and feeling the tears running down my face.

'What a waste of good tears!' the other girls had told me when I cried in the dressing-room that night. And I heard myself saying out loud in an affected voice, 'Oh, the waste, the waste, the waste!'

But that did not last long.

'What's the time?' I thought, and because I wasn't sleepy any longer I sat down in the chair by the window, waiting for the clock outside to strike.

Mannequin

Twelve o'clock. Déjeuner chez Jeanne Veron, Place Vendôme.

Anna, dressed in the black cotton, chemise-like garment of the mannequin off duty was trying to find her way along dark passages and down complicated flights of stairs to the underground room where lunch was served.

She was shivering, for she had forgotten her coat, and the garment that she wore was very short, sleeveless, displaying her rose-coloured stockings to the knee. Her hair was flamingly and honestly red; her eyes, which were very gentle in expression, brown and heavily shadowed with kohl; her face small and pale under its professional rouge. She was fragile, like a delicate child, her arms pathetically thin. It was to her legs that she owed this dazzling, this incredible opportunity.

Madame Veron, white-haired with black eyes, incredibly distinguished, who had given them one sweeping glance, the glance of the connoisseur, smiled imperiously and engaged her at an exceedingly small salary. As a beginner, Madame explained, Anna could not expect more. She was to wear the jeune fille dresses. Another smile, another sharp glance.

Anna was conducted from the Presence by an underling who helped her to take off the frock she had worn temporarily for the interview. Aspirants for an engagement are always dressed in a model of the house.

She had spent yesterday afternoon in a delirium tempered by a feeling of exaggerated reality, and in buying the necessary make up. It had been such a forlorn hope, answering the advertisement.

The morning had been dreamlike. At the back of the

wonderfully decorated salons she had found an unexpected sombreness; the place, empty, would have been dingy and melancholy, countless puzzling corridors and staircases, a rabbit warren and a labyrinth. She despaired of ever finding her way.

In the mannequins' dressing-room she spent a shy hour making up her face – in an extraordinary and distinctive atmosphere of slimness and beauty; white arms and faces vivid with rouge; raucous voices and the smell of cosmetics; silken lingerie. Coldly critical glances were bestowed upon Anna's reflection in the glass. None of them looked at her directly.... A depressing room, taken by itself, bare and cold, a very inadequate conservatory for these human flowers. Saleswomen in black rushed in and out, talking in sharp voices; a very old woman hovered, helpful and shapeless, showing Anna where to hang her clothes, presenting to her the black garment that Anna was wearing, going to lunch. She smiled with professional motherliness, her little, sharp, black eyes travelling rapidly from la nouvelle's hair to her ankles and back again.

She was Madame Pecard, the dresser.

Before Anna had spoken a word she was called away by a small boy in buttons to her destination in one of the salons: there, under the eye of a vendeuse, she had to learn the way to wear the innocent and springlike air and garb of the jeune fille. Behind a yellow, silken screen she was hustled into a leather coat and paraded under the cold eyes of an American buyer. This was the week when the spring models are shown to important people from big shops all over Europe and America: the most critical week of the season.... The American buyer said that he would have that, but with an inch on to the collar and larger cuffs. In vain the saleswoman, in her best English with its odd Chicago accent, protested that that would completely ruin the chic of the model. The American buyer knew what he wanted and saw that he got it.

The vendeuse sighed, but there was a note of admiration in her voice. She respected Americans: they were not like the English, who, under the surface of annoying moroseness of manner, were notoriously timid and easy to turn round your finger.

'Was that all right?' Behind the screen one of the sales-women smiled encouragingly and nodded. The other shrugged her shoulders. She had small, close-set eyes, a long thin nose and tight lips of the regulation puce colour. Behind her silken screen Anna sat on a high white stool. She felt that she appeared charming and troubled. The white and gold of the salon suited her red hair.

A short morning. For the mannequin's day begins at ten and the process of making up lasts an hour. The friendly saleswoman volunteered the information that her name was Jeannine, that she was in the lingerie, that she considered Anna *rudement jolie*, that noon was Anna's lunch hour. She must go down the corridor and up those stairs, through the big salon then.... Anyone would tell her. But Anna, lost in the labyrinth, was too shy to ask her way. Besides, she was not sorry to have time to brace herself for the ordeal. She had reached the regions of utility and oilcloth: the decorative salons were far overhead. Then the smell of food – almost visible, it was so cloudlike and heavy – came to her nostrils, and high-noted, and sibilant, a buzz of conversation made her draw a deep breath. She pushed a door open.

She was in a big, very low-ceilinged room, all the floor space occupied by long wooden tables with no cloths.... She was sitting at the mannequins' table, gazing at a thick and hideous white china plate, a twisted tin fork, a wooden-handled stained knife, a tumbler so thick it seemed unbreakable.

There were twelve mannequins at Jeanne Veron's: six of them were lunching, the others still paraded, goddess-like, till their turn came for rest and refreshment. Each of the twelve was of a distinct and separate type: each of the twelve knew her type and kept to it, practising rigidly in clothing, manner, voice and conversation.

Round the austere table were now seated: Babette, the gamine, the traditional blonde enfant: Mona, tall and darkly beautiful, the femme fatale, the wearer of sumptuous evening gowns. Georgette was the garçonne: Simone with green eyes Anna knew instantly for a cat whom men would and did adore, a sleek, white, purring, long-lashed creature.... Eliane was the star of the collection.

Eliane was frankly ugly and it did not matter: no doubt

Lilith, from whom she was obviously descended, had been ugly too. Her hair was henna-tinted, her eyes small and black, her complexion bad under her thick make-up. Her hips were extraordinarily slim, her hands and feet exquisite, every movement she made was as graceful as a flower's in the wind. Her walk.... But it was her walk which made her the star there and earned her a salary quite fabulous for Madame Veron's, where large salaries were not the rule.... Her walk and her 'chic of the devil' which lit an expression of admiration in even the cold eyes of American buyers.

Eliane was a quiet girl, pleasant-mannered. She wore a ring with a beautiful emerald on one long, slim finger, and in her small eyes were both intelligence and mystery.

Madame Pecard, the dresser, was seated at the head of the mannequin's table, talking loudly, unlistened to, and gazing benevolently at her flock.

At other tables sat the sewing girls, pale-faced, black-frocked – the workers, heroically gay, but with the stamp of labour on them: and the saleswomen. The mannequins, with their sensual, blatant charms and their painted faces were watched covertly, envied and apart.

Babette the blonde enfant was next to Anna, and having started the conversation with a few good, round oaths at the quality of the sardines, announced proudly that she could speak English and knew London very well. She began to tell Anna the history of her adventures in the city of coldness, dark and fogs.... She had gone to a job as a mannequin in Bond Street and the villainous proprietor of the shop having tried to make love to her and she being rigidly virtuous, she had left. And another job, Anna must figure to herself, had been impossible to get, for she, Babette, was too small and slim for the Anglo-Saxon idea of a mannequin.

She stopped to shout in a loud voice to the woman who was serving: 'Hé, my old one, don't forget your little Babette....'

Opposite, Simone the cat and the sportive Georgette were having a low-voiced conversation about the triste-ness of a monsieur of their acquaintance. 'I said to him,' Georgette finished decisively, 'Nothing to be done, my rabbit. You have not looked at me well, little one. In my place would you not have done the same?'

She broke off when she realized that the others were listening, and smiled in a friendly way at Anna.

She too, it appeared, had ambitions to go to London because the salaries were so much better there. Was it difficult? Did they really like French girls? Parisiennes?

The conversation became general.

'The English boys are nice,' said Babette, winking one divinely candid eye. 'I had a chic type who used to take me to dinner at the Empire Palace. Oh, a pretty boy....'

'It is the most chic restaurant in London,' she added importantly.

The meal reached the stage of dessert. The other tables were gradually emptying; the mannequins all ordered very strong coffee, several a liqueur. Only Mona and Eliane remained silent; Eliane, because she was thinking of something else; Mona, because it was her type, her genre to be haughty.

Her hair swept away from her white, narrow forehead and her small ears: her long earrings nearly touching her shoulders, she sipped her coffe with a disdainful air. Only once, when the blonde enfant, having engaged in a passage of arms with the waitress and got the worst of it, was momentarily discomfited and silent, Mona narrowed her eyes and smiled an astonishingly cruel smile.

As soon as her coffee was drunk she got up and went out.

Anna produced a cigarette, and Georgette, perceiving instantly that here was the sportive touch, her genre, asked for one and lit it with a devil-may-care air. Anna eagerly passed her cigarettes round, but the Mère Pecard interfered weightily. It was against the rules of the house for the mannequins to smoke, she wheezed. The girls all lit their cigarettes and smoked. The Mère Pecard rumbled on: 'A caprice, my children. All the world knows that mannequins are capricious. Is it not so?' She appealed to the rest of the room.

As they went out Babette put her arm round Anna's waist and whispered: 'Don't answer Madame Pecard. We don't like her. We never talk to her. She spies on us. She is a camel.'

That afternoon Anna stood for an hour to have a dress draped on her. She showed this dress to a stout Dutch lady buying for the Hague, to a beautiful South American with pearls, to a silver-haired American gentleman who wanted an evening cape for his daughter of seventeen, and to a hook-nosed, odd English lady of title who had a loud voice and dressed, under her furs, in a grey jersey and stout boots.

The American gentleman approved of Anna, and said so, and Anna gave him a passionately grateful glance. For, if the vendeuse Jeannine had been uniformly kind and encouraging, the other, Madame Tienne, had been as uniformly disapproving and had once even pinched her arm hard.

About five o'clock Anna became exhausted. The four white and gold walls seemed to close in on her. She sat on her high white stool staring at a marvellous nightgown and fighting an intense desire to rush away. Anywhere! Just to dress and rush away anywhere, from the raking eyes of the customers and the pinching fingers of Irene.

'I will one day. I can't stick it,' she said to herself. 'I won't be able to stick it.' She had an absurd wish to gasp for air.

Jeannine came and found her like that.

'It is hard at first, hein?… One asks oneself: Why? For what good? It is all idiot. We are all so. But we go on. Do not worry about Irene.' She whispered: Madame Veron likes you very much. I heard her say so.'

At six o'clock Anna was out in the rue de la Paix; her fatigue forgotten, the feeling that now she really belonged to the great, maddening city possessed her and she was happy in her beautifully cut tailor-made and a beret.

Georgette passed her and smiled; Babette was in a fur coat.

All up the street the mannequins were coming out of the shops, pausing on the pavements a moment, making them as gay and as beautiful as beds of flowers before they walked swiftly away and the Paris night swallowed them up.

A Night

One shuts one's eyes and sees it written: red letters on a black ground:

Le Saut dans l'Inconnu…. Le Saut….

Stupidly I think: But why in French? Of course it must be a phrase I have read somewhere. Idiotic.

I screw up my eyes wildly to get rid of it: next moment it is back again.

Red letters on a black ground.

One lies staring at the exact shape of the S.

Dreadfully tired I am too, now this beastly thing won't let me sleep. And because I can't sleep I start to think very slowly and painfully, for I have cried myself into a state of stupor.

No money: rotten. And ill and frightened to death…. Worse!

But worst of all is the way I hate people: it is as if something in me is shivering right away from humanity. Their eyes are mean and cruel, especially when they laugh.

They are always laughing, too: always grinning. When they say something especially rotten they grin. Then, just for a second, that funny little animal, the Real Person, looks out and slinks away again…. Furtive.

I don't belong here. I don't belong here. I must get out –must get out.

Le Saut…. Le Saut dans l'Inconnu.

One lies very still – staring.

Well, then…what?

Make a hole in the water?

In a minute I am sitting up in bed, gasping. I have imagined myself sinking, suffocating, the pain in the lungs horrible.

Horrible.

Shoot oneself?… I begin again mechanically to plan what would happen. The revolver is in the pawnshop. For twenty francs I could….

I'd sit down. No: lie down. And open my mouth…. That's the place: against the roof of one's mouth. How rum it would feel. And pull the trigger.

And then?

L'Inconnu: black, awful. One would fall, down, down, down for ever and ever. Falling.

Frightened. Coward. Do it when you hardly know. Drink perhaps first half a bottle of Cognac.

No: I cannot put up a better fight than that…. *Be* ashamed of me.

If I had something to hold on to. Or somebody.

One friend…. One!

You know I can't be alone. I can't.

God, send me a friend….

How ridiculous I am. How primitive….

Sneering at myself I start on childishnesses.

I imagine the man I could love. His hands, eyes and voice.

Hullo, he'll say, what's all this fuss about?

– Because I'm hurt and spoilt, and you too late….

– What rot…. What rot!

He will buy me roses and carnations and chocolates and a pair of pink silk pyjamas and heaps of books.

He will laugh and say – but nicely:

Finished! What rot!

Just like that.

Saying the Litany to the Blessed Virgin which I learnt at the Convent and have never forgotten.

Mater Dolorosa: Mother most sorrowful. Pray for us, Star of the Sea. Mother most pitiful, pray for us.

Ripping words.

I wonder if I dare shut my eyes now.

Ridiculous all this. Lord, I am tired….

A devil of a business….

La Grosse Fifi

'The sea,' said Mark Olsen, 'is exactly the colour of Reckitt's blue this morning.'

Roseau turned her head to consider the smooth Mediterranean.

'I like it like that,' she announced, 'and I wish you wouldn't walk so fast. I loathe tearing along, and this road wasn't made to tear along anyhow.'

'Sorry,' said Mark, 'just a bad habit.'

They walked in silence, Mark thinking that this girl was a funny one, but he'd rather like to see a bit more of her. A pity Peggy seemed to dislike her – women were rather a bore with their likes and dislikes.

'Here's my hotel,' said the funny one. 'Doesn't it look awful?'

'You know,' Mark told her seriously, 'you really oughtn't to stay here. It's a dreadful place. Our patronne says that it's got a vile reputation – someone got stabbed or something, and the patron went to jail.'

'You don't say!' mocked Roseau.

'I do say. There's a room going at the pension.'

'Hate pensions.'

'Well, move then, move to St Paul or Juan les Pins – Peggy was saying yesterday....'

'Oh Lord!' said Roseau rather impatiently, 'my hotel's all right. I'll move when I'm ready, when I've finished some work I'm doing. I think I'll go back to Paris – I'm getting tired of the Riviera, it's too tidy. Will you come in and have an aperitif?'

Her tone was so indifferent that Mark, piqued, accepted the invitation though the restaurant of that hotel really depressed him. It was so dark, so gloomy, so full of odd-looking, very odd-looking French people with abnormally loud voices even for French people. A faint odour of garlic floated in the air.

'Have a Deloso,' said Roseau. 'It tastes of anis,' she explained, seeing that he looked blank. 'It's got a kick in it.'

'Thank you,' said Mark. He put his sketches carefully on the table, then looking over Roseau's head his eyes became astonished and fixed. He said: 'Oh my Lord! What's that?'

'That's Fifi,' answered Roseau in a low voice and relaxing into a smile for the first time.

'Fifi! Of course – it would be – Good Lord! – Fifi!' His voice was awed. 'She's – she's terrific, isn't she?'

'She's a dear,' said Roseau unexpectedly.

Fifi was not terrific except metaphorically, but she was stout, well corseted – her stomach carefully arranged to form part of her chest. Her hat was large and worn with a rakish sideways slant, her rouge shrieked, and the lids of her protruding eyes were painted bright blue. She wore very long silver earrings; nevertheless her face looked huge – vast, and her voice was hoarse though there was nothing but Vichy water in her glass.

Her small, plump hands were covered with rings, her small, plump feet encased in very high-heeled, patent leather shoes.

Fifi was obvious in fact – no mistaking her mission in life. With her was a young man of about twenty-four. He would have been a handsome young man had he not plastered his face with white powder and worn his hair in a high mass above his forehead.

'She reminds me,' said Mark in a whisper, 'of Max Beerbohm's picture of the naughty lady considering Edward VII's head on a coin – You know, the "Ah! well, he'll always be Tum-Tum to me" one.'

'Yes,' said Roseau, 'she is Edwardian, isn't she?' For some unexplainable reason she disliked these jeers at Fifi, resented them even more than she resented most jeers. After all the lady looked so good-natured, such a good sort, her laugh was so jolly.

She said: 'Haven't you noticed what lots there are down here? Edwardian ladies, I mean – Swarms in Nice, shoals in Monte Carlo! – In the Casino the other day I saw…'

'Who's the gentleman?' Mark asked, not to be diverted. 'Her son?'

'Her son?' said Roseau, 'Good Heavens, no! That's her gigolo.'

'Her – what did you say?'

'Her gigolo,' explained Roseau coldly. 'Don't you know what a gigolo is? They exist in London, I assure you. She keeps him – he makes love to her, I know all about it because their room's next to mine.'

'Oh!' muttered Mark. He began to sip his aperitif hastily.

'I love your name anyway,' he said, changing the conversation abruptly – 'It suits you.'

'Yes, it suits me – it means a reed,' said Roseau. She had a queer smile – a little sideways smile. Mark wasn't quite sure that he liked it – 'A reed shaken by the wind. That's my motto, that is – are you going? Yes, I'll come to tea soon – sometime: goodbye!'

'He's running off to tell his wife how right she was about me,' thought Roseau, watching him. 'How rum some English people are! They ask to be shocked and long to be shocked and hope to be shocked, but if you really shock them…how shocked they are!'

She finished her aperitif gloomily. She was waiting for an American acquaintance who was calling to take her to lunch. Meanwhile the voices of Fifi and the gigolo grew louder.

'I tell you,' said the gigolo, 'that I must go to Nice this afternoon. It is necessary – I am forced.'

His voice was apologetic but sullen, with a hint of the bully. The male straining at his bonds.

'But, mon chéri,' implored Fifi, 'may I not come with you? We will take tea at the Negresco afterwards.'

The gigolo was sulkily silent. Obviously the Negresco with Fifi did not appeal to him.

She gave way at once.

'Marie!' she called, 'serve Monsieur immediately. Monsieur must catch the one-thirty to Nice…. You will return to dinner, my Pierrot?' she begged huskily.

'I think so, I will see,' answered the gigolo loftily, following up his victory as all good generals should – and at that moment Roseau's American acquaintance entered the restaurant.

They lunched on the terrace of a villa looking down on the calmly smiling sea.

'That blue, that blue!' sighed Miss Ward, for such was the American lady's name – 'I always say that blue's wonderful. It gets right down into one's soul – don't you think, Mr Wheeler?'

Mr Wheeler turned his horn spectacles severely on the blue.

'Very fine,' he said briefly.

'I'm sure,' thought Roseau, 'that he's wondering how much it would sell for – bottled.'

She found herself thinking of a snappy advertisement: 'Try our Bottled Blue for Soul Ills.'

Then pulling herself together she turned to Mr Leroy, the fourth member of the party, who was rapidly becoming sulky.

Monsieur Leroy was what the French call 'un joli garçon' – he was even, one might say, a very pretty boy indeed – tall, broad, tanned, clean looking as any Anglo-Saxon. Yet for quite three-quarters of an hour two creatures of the female sex had taken not the faintest notice of him. Monsieur Leroy was puzzled, incredulous. Now he began to be annoyed.

However, he responded instantly to Roseau's effort to include him in the conversation.

'Oh, Madame,' he said, 'I must say that very strong emotion is an excuse for anything – one is mad for the moment.'

'There!' said Roseau in triumph, for the argument had been about whether anything excused the Breaking of Certain Rules.

'That's all nonsense,' said Mr Wheeler.

'But you excuse a sharp business deal?' persisted Roseau.

'Business,' said Mr Wheeler, as if speaking to a slightly idiotic child, 'is quite different, Miss…er….'

'You think that,' argued Roseau, 'because it's your form of emotion.'

Mr Wheeler gave her up.

'Maurice,' said Miss Ward, who loved peace, to the young Frenchman, 'fetch the gramophone, there's a good child!'

The gramophone was fetched and the strains of 'Lady, be Good' floated out towards the blue.

The hotel seemed sordid that night to Roseau, full of gentlemen in caps and loudly laughing females. There were large lumps of garlic in the food, the wine was sour…. She felt very tired, bruised, aching, yet dull as if she had been defeated in some fierce struggle.

'Oh God, I'm going to think, don't let me think,' she prayed.

For two weeks she had desperately fought off thoughts. She drank another glass of wine, looked at Fifi sitting alone at the mimosa-decorated table with protruding eyes fixed on the door; then looked away again as though the sight frightened her. Her dinner finished she went straight up into her bedroom, took three cachets of veronal, undressed, lay down with the sheet over her head.

Suddenly she got up, staggered against the table, said 'Damn', turned the light on and began to dress, but quietly, quietly. Out through the back door. And why was she dressing anyway? Never mind – done now. And who the hell was that knocking?

It was Fifi. She was wonderfully garbed in a transparent nightgown of a vivid rose colour trimmed with yellow lace. Over this she had hastily thrown a dirty dressing-gown, knotting the sleeves round her neck.

She stared at Roseau, her eyes full of a comic amazement.

'I hope I do not disturb you, Madame,' she said politely. 'But I heard you – enfin – I was afraid that you were ill. My room is next door.'

'It is?' said Roseau faintly. She felt giddy and clutched at the corner of the table.

'You are surely not thinking of going out now,' Fifi remarked. 'I think it is almost midnight, and you do not look well, Madame.'

She spoke gently, coaxingly, and put her hand on Roseau's arm.

Roseau collapsed on the bed in a passion of tears.

'Ma petite,' said Fifi with decision, 'you will be better in bed, believe me. Where is your chemise de nuit? Ah!'

She took it from the chair close by, looked rapidly with a calculating eye at the lace on it, then put a firm hand on Roseau's skirt to help her with the process of undressing.

'La,' she said, giving the pillow a pat, 'and here is your pocket handkerchief.'

She was not dismayed, contemptuous or curious. She was comforting.

'To cry is good,' she remarked after a pause. 'But not too
much. Can I get anything for you, my little one? Some hot milk
with rum in it?'

'No, no,' said Roseau, clutching the flannel sleeve, 'don't go
– don't leave me – lonely –'

She spoke in English, but Fifi responding at once to the
appeal answered:

'Pauvre chou – va,' and bent down to kiss her.

It seemed to Roseau the kindest, the most understanding
kiss she had ever had, and comforted she watched Fifi sit on
the foot of the bed and wrap her flannel dressing-gown more
closely round her. Mistily she imagined that she was a child
again and that this was a large, protecting person who would
sit there till she slept.

The bed creaked violently under the lady's weight.

'Cursed bed,' muttered Fifi. 'Everything in this house is
broken, and then the prices they charge! It is shameful....'

'I am very unhappy,' remarked Roseau in French in a small,
tired voice. Her swollen eyelids were half shut.

'And do you think I have not seen?' said Fifi earnestly,
laying one plump hand on Roseau's knee. 'Do you think I
don't know when a woman is unhappy? – I – Besides, with you
it is easy to see. You look avec les yeux d'une biche – It's
naturally a man who makes you unhappy?'

'Yes,' said Roseau. To Fifi she could tell everything – Fifi was
as kind as God.

'Ah! le salaud: ah! le monstre.' This was said mechanically,
without real indignation. 'Men are worth nothing. But why
should he make you unhappy? He is perhaps jealous?'

'Oh, no!' said Roseau.

'Then perhaps he is méchant – there are men like that – or
perhaps he is trying to disembarrass himself of you.'

'That's it,' said Roseau, 'He is trying to – disembarrass
himself of me.'

'Ah!' said Fifi wisely. She leant closer. 'Mon enfant,' said she
hoarsely, 'do it first. Put him at the door with a coup de pied
quelque part.'

'But I haven't got a door,' said Roseau in English, beginning
to laugh hysterically. 'No vestige of a door I haven't – no door,
no house, no friends, no money, no nothing.'

'Comment?' said Fifi suspiciously. She disliked foreign languages being talked in her presence.

'Supposing I do – what then?' Roseau asked her.

'What then?' screamed Fifi. 'You ask what then – you who are pretty. If I were in your place I would not ask "what then", I tell you – I should find a chic type – and quickly!'

'Oh!' said Roseau. She was beginning to feel drowsy.

'Un clou chasse l'autre,' remarked Fifi, rather gloomily. 'Yes, that is life – one nail drives out the other nail.'

She got up.

'One says that.' Her eyes were melancholy. 'But when one is caught it is not so easy. No, I adore my Pierrot. I adore that child – I would give him my last sou – and how can he love me? I am old, I am ugly. Oh, I know. Regarde moi ces yeux là!' She pointed to the caverns under her eyes – 'Et ça!' She touched her enormous chest. 'Pierrot who only loves slim women. Que voulez-vous?'

Fifi's shrug was wonderful!

'I love him – I bear everything. But what a life! What a life!… You, my little one, a little courage – we will try to find you a chic type, a –'

She stopped seeing that Roseau was almost asleep. 'Alors – I am going – sleep well.'

Next morning Roseau, with a dry tongue, a heavy head, woke to the sound of loud voices in the next room.

Fifi, arguing, grumbling, finally weeping – the gigolo who had obviously just come in, protesting, becoming surly.

'Menteur, menteur, you have been with a woman!'

'I tell you no. You make ideas for yourself.'

Sobs, kisses, a reconciliation.

'Oh Lord! Oh Lord!' said Roseau. She put the friendly sheet over her head thinking: 'I must get out of this place.'

But when an hour afterwards the stout lady knocked and made her appearance she was powdered, smiling and fresh – almost conventional.

'I hope you slept well last night, Madame; I hope you feel better this morning? Can I do anything for you?'

'Yes, sit and talk to me,' said Roseau, 'I'm not getting up this morning.'

'You are right,' Fifi answered. 'That reposes, a day in bed.'

She sat heavily down and beamed. 'And then you must amuse yourself a little,' she advised. 'Distract yourself. If you wish I will show you all the places where one amuses oneself in Nice.'

But Roseau, who saw the 'chic type' lurking in Fifi's eyes, changed the conversation. She said she wished she had something to read.

'I will lend you a book,' said Fifi at once. 'I have many books.'

She went to her room and came back with a thin volume.

'Oh, poetry!' said Roseau. She had hoped for a good detective story. She did not feel in the mood for French poetry.

'I adore poetry,' said Fifi with sentiment. 'Besides, this is very beautiful. You understand French perfectly? Then listen.'

She began to read:

> *'Dans le chemin libre de mes années*
> *Je marchais fière et je me suis arrêtée....*
> ....
> *'Thou hast bound my ankles with silken cords.*
> ....
> *'Que j'oublie les mots qui ne disent pas mon amour,*
> *Les gestes qui ne doivent pas t'enlacer,*
> *Que l'horizon se ferme à ton sourire....*
> ....
> *'Mais je t'en conjure, ô Sylvius, comme la plus humble des choses*
> *qui ont une place dans ta maison – garde-moi.'*

In other words: you won't be rotten – now. Will you, will you? I'll do anything you like, but be kind to me, won't you, won't you?

Not that it didn't sound better in French.

'Now,' read Fifi,

> *'I can walk lightly for I have laid my life in the hands of my lover.*
> ....
> *'Chante, chante ma vie, aux mains de mon amant!'*

And so on, and so on.

Roseau thought that it was horrible to hear this ruin of a woman voicing all her own moods, all her own thoughts. Horrible.

'*Sylvius, que feras-tu à travers les jours de cet*
être que t'abandonne sa faiblesse?
Il peut vivre d'un sourire, mourir d'une parole.
Sylvius, qu'en feras-tu?'

'Have you got any detective stories?' Roseau interrupted suddenly. She felt that she could not bear any more.

Fifi was surprised but obliging. Yes – she had Arsène Lupin, several of Gaston Leroux; also she had 'Shaerlock 'Olmes'.

Roseau chose *Le Fantôme de l'Opéra*, and when Fifi had left the room, stared for a long time at the same page:

'*Sylvius, qu'en feras-tu?*'

Suddenly she started to laugh and she laughed long, and very loudly for Roseau, who had a small voice and the ghost of a laugh.

That afternoon Roseau met Sylvius, alias the gigolo, in the garden of the hotel.

She had made up her mind to detest him. What excuse for the gigolo? None – none whatever.

There he was with his mistress in Cannes and his mistress in Nice. And Fifi on the rack. Fifi, with groans, producing a billet de mille when the gigolo turned the screw. Horrible gigolo!

She scowled at him, carefully thinking out a gibe about the colour of his face powder. But that afternoon his face was unpowdered and reluctantly she was forced to see that the creature was handsome. There was nothing of the blond beast about the gigolo – he was dark, slim, beautiful as some Latin god. And how soft his eyes were, how sweet his mouth....

Horrible, horrible gigolo!

He did not persist, but looking rather surprised at her snub, went away with a polite murmer: 'Alors, Madame.'

A week later he disappeared.

Fifi in ten days grew ten years older and she came no more to Roseau's room to counsel rum and hot milk instead of veronal. But head up, she faced a hostile and sneering world.

'Have you any news of Monsieur Rivière?' the patronne of

the hotel would ask with a little cruel female smile.

'Oh, yes, he is very well,' Fifi would answer airily, knowing perfectly well that the patronne had already examined her letters carefully. 'His grandmother, alas! is much worse, poor woman.'

For the gigolo had chosen the illness of his grandmother as a pretext for his abrupt departure.

One day Fifi despatched by post a huge wreath of flowers – it appeared that the gigolo's grandmother had departed this life.

Then silence. No thanks for the flowers.

Fifi's laugh grew louder and hoarser, and she gave up Vichy for champagne.

She was no longer alone at her table – somehow she could collect men – and as she swam into the room like a big vessel with all sails set, three, four, five would follow in her wake, the party making a horrible noise.

'That dreadful creature!' said Peggy Olsen one night. 'How does she get all those men together?'

Mark laughed and said: 'Take care, she's a pal of Roseau's.'

'Oh! is she?' said Mrs Olsen. She disliked Roseau and thought the hotel with its clientèle of chauffeurs – and worse – beyond what an English gentlewoman should be called upon to put up with.

She was there that night because her husband had insisted on it.

'The girl's lonely – come on, Peggy – don't be such a wet blanket.'

So Peggy had gone, her tongue well sharpened, ready for the fray.

'The dear lady must be very rich,' she remarked. 'She's certainly most hospitable.'

'Oh, she isn't the hostess,' said Roseau, absurdly anxious that her friend's triumph should be obvious. 'The man with the beard is host, I'm sure. He adores Fifi.'

'Extraordinary!' said Mrs Olsen icily.

Roseau thought: 'You sneering beast, you little sneering beast. Fifi's worth fifty of you!' – but she said nothing, contenting herself with one of those sideways smiles which made people think: 'She's a funny one.'

The electric light went out.

The thin, alert, fatigued-looking bonne brought candles. That long drab room looked ghostly in the flickering light – one had an oddly definite impression of something sinister and dangerous – all these heavy jowls and dark, close-set eyes, coarse hands, loud, quarrelsome voices. Fifi looked sinister too with her vital hair and ruined throat.

'You know,' Roseau said suddenly, 'you're right. My hotel is a rum place.'

'Rum is a good word,' said Mark Olsen. 'You really oughtn't to stay here.'

'No, I'm going to leave. It's just been sheer laziness to make the move and my room is rather charming. There's a big mimosa tree just outside the window. But I will leave.'

As the electric light came on again they were discussing the prices of various hotels.

But next morning Roseau, lying in bed and staring at the mimosa tree, faced the thought of how much she would miss Fifi.

It was ridiculous, absurd, but there it was. Just the sound of that hoarse voice always comforted her; gave her the sensation of being protected, strengthened.

'I must be dotty,' said Roseau to herself. 'Of course I would go and like violently someone like that – I must be dotty. No, I'm such a coward, so dead frightened of life, that I must hang on to somebody – even Fifi....'

Dead frightened of life was Roseau, suspended over a dark and terrible abyss – the abyss of absolute loss of self-control.

'Fifi,' said Roseau talking to herself, 'is a pal. She cheers me up. On the other hand she's a dreadful-looking old tart, and I oughtn't to go about with her. It'll be another good old Downward Step if I do.'

Fifi knocked.

She was radiant, bursting with some joyful tidings.

'Pierrot is returning,' she announced.

'Oh!' said Roseau interested.

'Yes, I go to meet him at Nice this afternoon.'

'I am glad!' said Roseau.

It was impossible not to be glad in that large and beaming presence. Fifi wore a new black frock with lace at the neck and wrists and a new hat, a small one.

'My hat?' she said anxiously. 'Does it make me ridiculous? Is it too small? Does it make me look old?'

'No,' said Roseau, considering her carefully – 'I like it, but put the little veil down.'

Fifi obeyed.

'Ah, well,' she sighed, 'I was always ugly. When I was small my sister called me the devil's doll. Yes – always the compliments like that are what I get. now – alas! You are sure I am not ridiculous in that hat?'

'No, no,' Roseau told her. 'You look very nice.'

Dinner that night was a triumph for Fifi – champagne flowed – three bottles of it. An enormous bunch of mimosa and carnations almost hid the table from view. The patronne looked sideways, half enviously; the patron chuckled, and the gigolo seemed pleased and affable.

Roseau drank her coffee and smoked a cigarette at the festive table, but refused to accompany them to Nice. They were going to a boîte de nuit, 'all that was of the most chic'.

'Ah bah!' said Fifi good-naturedly scornful, 'she is droll the little one. She always wishes to hide in a corner like a little mouse.'

'No one,' thought Roseau, awakened at four in the morning, 'could accuse Fifi of being a little mouse.' Nothing of the mouse about Fifi.

'I'm taking him to Monte Carlo,' the lady announced next morning. She pronounced it Monte Carl'.

'Monte Carlo – why?'

'He wishes to go. Ah! la la – it will cost me something!' She made a little rueful, clucking noise. 'And Pierrot, who always gives such large tips to the waiters – if he knew as I do what salauds are the garçons de café –'

'Well, enjoy yourself,' Roseau said laughing. 'Have a good time.'

The next morning she left the hotel early and did not return till dinnertime, late, preoccupied.

As she began her meal she noticed that some men in the restaurant were jabbering loudly in Italian – but they always jabbered.

The patron was not there – the patronne, looking haughty, was talking rapidly to her lingère.

But the bonne looked odd, Roseau thought, frightened but bursting with importance. As she reached the kitchen she called in a shrill voice to the cook: 'It is in the *Éclaireur*. Have you seen?'

Roseau finished peeling her apple. Then she called out to the patronne – she felt impelled to do it.

'What is it, Madame? Has anything happened?'

The patronne hesitated.

'Madame Carly – Madame Fifi – has met with an accident,' she answered briefly.

'An accident? An automobile accident? Oh, I do hope it isn't serious.'

'It's serious enough – assez grave,' the patronne answered evasively.

Roseau asked no more questions. She took up the *Éclaireur de Nice* lying on the table and looked through it.

She was looking for the 'Fatal Automobile Accident'.

She found the headline:

YET ANOTHER DRAMA OF JEALOUSY

'Madame Francine Carly, aged 48, of 7 rue Notre Dame des Pleurs, Marseilles, was fatally stabbed last night at the hotel—, Monte Carlo, by her lover Pierre Rivière, aged 24, of rue Madame Tours. Questioned by the police he declared that he acted in self-defence as his mistress, who was of a very jealous temperament, had attacked him with a knife when told of his approaching marriage, and threatened to blind him. When the proprietor of the hotel, alarmed by the woman's shrieks, entered the room accompanied by two policemen, Madame Carly was lying unconscious, blood streaming from the wounds in her throat. She was taken to the hospital, where she died without recovering consciousness.

'The murderer has been arrested and taken to the Dépôt.'

Roseau stared for a long time at the paper.

'I must leave this hotel,' was her only thought, and she slept soundly that night without fear of ghosts.

A horrible, sordid business. Poor Fifi! Almost she hated

herself for feeling so little regret.

But next morning while she was packing she opened the book of poems, slim, much handled, still lying on the table, and searched for the verse Fifi had read:

> *'Maintenant je puis marcher légère,*
> *J'ai mis toute ma vie aux mains de mon amant.*
> *Chante, chante ma vie aux mains de mon amant.'*

Suddenly Roseau began to cry.

'O poor Fifi! O poor Fifi!'

In that disordered room in the midst of her packing she cried bitterly, heartbroken.

Till, in the yellow sunshine that streamed into the room, she imagined that she saw her friend's gay and childlike soul, freed from its gross body, mocking her gently for her sentimental tears.

'Oh well!' said Roseau.

She dried her eyes and went on with her packing.

Trio

They sat at a corner table in the little restaurant, eating with gusto and noise after the manner of simple-hearted people who like their neighbours to see and know their pleasures.

The man was very black – coal black, with a thick silver ring on a finger of one hand. He wore a smart grey lounge suit, cut in at the waist, and his woolly hair was carefully brushed back and brilliantined. The woman was coffee-coloured and fat. She had on the native Martinique turban, making no pretension to fashion. Her bodice and skirt gaped apart and through the opening a coarse white cotton chemise peeped innocently forth…. From the Antilles….

Between them was the girl, apparently about fifteen, but probably much younger. She sat very close to the man and every now and then would lay her head on his shoulder for a second…. There was evidently much white blood in her veins: the face was charming.

She had exactly the movements of a very graceful kitten, and he, appreciative, would stop eating to kiss her…long, lingering kisses, and, after each one she would look round the room as if to gather up a tribute of glances of admiration and envy – a lovely, vicious little thing…. From the Antilles, too. You cannot think what home-sickness descended over me….

The fuzzy, negress' hair was exactly the right frame for her vulgar, impudent, startlingly alive little face: the lips were just thick enough to be voluptuous, the eyes with an expression half cunning, half intelligent. She wore a very short red frock and black, patent leather shoes. Her legs were bare. Suddenly she began to sing: *J'en ai marre*, to the huge delight of the coal black man who applauded vigorously.

As she grew more excited she jumped up, swung her slim

hips violently, rolled her eyes, stamped her feet, lifted her skirt. Obviously the red dress was her only garment, obviously too she was exquisite beneath it...supple, slender, a dancer from the Thousand and One Nights....

J'en ai m-a-r-r-e.

The fat, coffee-coloured woman looked on peacefully, then, after a cautious glance at the patronne seated behind her counter:

'Keep yourself quiet, Doudou,' she said. 'Keep yourself quiet.' Then with a happy laugh:

'Mais...ce qu'elle est cocasse, quand même!' she said proudly.

It was because these were my compatriots that in that Montparnasse restaurant I remembered the Antilles.

Again the Antilles

The editor of the *Dominica Herald and Leeward Islands Gazette* lived in a tall, white house with green Venetian blinds which overlooked our garden. I used often to see him looking solemnly out of his windows and would gaze solemnly back, for I though him a very awe-inspiring person.

He wore gold-rimmed spectacles and dark clothes always – not for him the frivolity of white linen even on the hottest day – a stout little man of a beautiful shade of coffee-colour, he was known throughout the Island as Papa Dom.

A born rebel, this editor: a firebrand. He hated the white people, not being quite white, and he despised the black ones, not being quite black…. 'Coloured' we West Indians call the intermediate shades, and I used to think that being coloured embittered him.

He was against the Government, against the English, against the Island's being a Crown Colony and the Town Board's new system of drainage. He was also against the Mob, against the gay and easy morality of the negroes and 'the horde of priests and nuns that overrun our unhappy Island', against the existence of the Anglican bishop and the Catholic bishop's new palace.

He wrote seething articles against that palace which was then being built, partly by voluntary labour – until, one night his house was besieged by a large mob of the faithful, throwing stones and howling for his blood. He appeared on his verandah, frightened to death. In the next issue of his paper he wrote a long account of the 'riot': according to him it had been led by several well-known Magdalenes, then, as always, the most ardent supporters of Christianity.

After that, though, he let the Church severely alone,

acknowledging that it was too strong for him.

I cannot imagine what started the quarrel between himself and Mr Hugh Musgrave.

Mr Hugh Musgrave I regarded as a dear, but peppery. Twenty years of the tropics and much indulgence in spices and cocktails does have that effect. He owned a big estate, just outside the town of Roseau, cultivated limes and sugar canes and employed a great deal of labour, but he was certainly neither ferocious nor tyrannical.

Suddenly, however, there was the feud in full swing.

There was in the *Dominica Herald and Leeward Islands Gazette* a column given up to letters from readers and, in this column, writing under the pseudonyms of Pro Patria, Indignant, Liberty and Uncle Tom's Cabin, Papa Dom let himself go. He said what he thought about Mr Musgrave and Mr Musgrave replied: briefly and sternly as befits an Englishman of the governing class.... Still he replied.

It was most undignified, but the whole Island was hugely delighted. Never had the *Herald* had such a sale.

Then Mr Musgrave committed, according to Papa Dom, some specially atrocious act of tyranny. Perhaps he put a fence up where he should not have, or overpaid an unpopular overseer or supported the wrong party on the Town Board.... At any rate Papa Dom wrote in the next issue of the paper this passionate and unforgettable letter:

'It is a saddening and a dismal sight,' it ended, 'to contemplate the degeneracy of a stock. How far is such a man removed from the ideas of true gentility, from the beautiful description of a contemporary, possibly, though not certainly, the Marquis of Montrose, left us by Shakespeare, the divine poet and genius.

'*He was a very gentle, perfect knight....*'

Mr Musgrave took his opportunity:

'Dear Sir,' he wrote,

'I never read your abominable paper. But my attention has been called to a scurrilous letter about myself which you published last week. The lines quoted were written, not by

Shakespeare but by Chaucer, though you cannot of course be
expected to know that, and run

> *He never yet no vilonye had sayde*
> *In al his lyf, unto no manner of wight –*
> *He was a verray parfit, gentil knyght.*

'It is indeed a saddening and a dismal thing that the names
of great Englishmen should be thus taken in vain by the
ignorant of another race and colour.'
Mr Musgrave had really written 'damn niggers'.

Papa Dom was by no means crushed. Next week he replied
with dignity as follows:

'My attention has been called to your characteristic letter. I
accept your correction though I understand that in the mind of
the best authorities there are grave doubts, very grave doubts
indeed, as to the authorship of the lines, and indeed the other
works of the immortal Swan of Avon. However, as I do not
write with works of reference in front of me, as you most
certainly do, I will not dispute the point.

'The conduct of an English gentleman who stoops to acts of
tyranny and abuse cannot be described as gentle or perfect. I
fail to see that it matters whether it is Shakespeare, Chaucer or
the Marquis of Montrose who administers from down the ages
the much-needed reminder and rebuke.'

I wonder if I shall ever again read the *Dominica Herald and
Leeward Islands Gazette*.

The Bishop's Feast

When I'd left Dominica twenty-five years ago there were no hotels, only a small boarding-house run by three sisters. The few people who wished to stay usually rented a house. So I was relieved when I saw the large cool room in the La Paz. There was a bathroom, and flush lavatories. All was well.

The next morning one of my mother's old friends sent me some flowers, and there was a letter from Mother Mount Calvary, the Mother Superior of the convent where I was at school, whom I had loved so much. She wrote 'Welcome back to Dominica. Come to see us at 4 o'clock this afternoon. How could I forget you?'

I asked the driver of the car we had hired to take me to the convent. He told me the old convent I knew had been sold, and the nuns were now living in a much smaller building. They would soon be going back to England and would be replaced by nuns of a Belgian order. 'I hear the old nun says she won't go, but she'll soon find out that she has to.'

'Isn't it rather a shame,' I said, 'to make them leave when they've worked so hard here, all their lives?'

He said 'They're too old for the job, anyway.'

Mother Mount Calvary – Good Mother, we used to call her – was smiling when she welcomed me and looked almost as cheerful as I remembered her. When she stopped smiling I saw that her face was very sombre and old. We sat in the garden with two other nuns who I thought I didn't know. One of them remarked how much I had changed.

'She hasn't changed at all,' Mother Mount Calvary said sharply.

When I looked again at the nun I recognized something in

her expression. She was the little Irish nun I had once seen smiling at her reflection in a barrel of water. There were no dimples now. She was a frightened old lady.

So this was the end of the feud between the convent and the bishopric, which had started at the new bishop's feast.

We'd all subscribed towards a present for the new bishop. It was an armchair to be given to him when he came to watch the performance celebrating his feast. We were excited about this performance.

The evening came. We clustered in the wings listening to a girl reciting *'Partant pour la Syrie,'* which was the first item on the programme. She didn't seem at all nervous. Her voice sounded clear and assured:

> *'Partant pour la Syrie le jeune et beau Dunois*
> *Venait prier Marie de bénir ses exploits.*
> *"Faites, Reine Immortelle," lui dit-il en partant,*
> *"Que j'aime la plus belle et sois le plus vaillant."'*

Louise was dressed for her song *'L'Anglaise à Paris'*, a mild satire on Englishwomen in Paris and the next item, when Mother St Edmund came bustling in and without giving us any reason told us that the programme had been changed. *'L'Anglaise à Paris'* was cancelled, instead a selected chorus was to sing 'Killarney'.

Consternation, giggles.

'Don't be silly, children,' said Mother St Edmund. 'Sing up and do your best. You all know the words.'

'He won't like that one either,' said Mother Sacred Heart. But Mother St Edmund urged us on:

> *'By Killarney's lakes and fells,*
> *Emerald isles and winding bays....'*

From the stage we could see the bishop enthroned in his new armchair, Mother Mount Calvary by his side. A large audience of parents and friends stretched away to the end of the room.

> *'...Beauty's home, Killarney.*
> *Heaven's reflex, Killarney.'*

The curtain came down.

Somebody played a Chopin mazurka and everything went more or less smoothly on to a series of tableaux vivants, the most important part of the programme.

The first one was of the Last Supper with Mary Magdalene at the feet of Christ. None of the apostles appeared. Delia Paulson's hair was exactly right – she played Mary Magdalene – though her face, which was hidden, wouldn't have done at all. Mildred Watts was Jesus Christ. She was lovely, just like Jesus. The nuns had fixed her up with a little beard and she looked into the distance over Mary's head. (I thought Christ might have looked at Mary but I suppose the nuns told Mildred not to.) However, His hand was raised in a rather absentminded blessing.

The next tableau was the Death of St Cecilia, patron saint of music. There was a statue of her above the piano on which I practised and I always thought she looked at me most severely when I played the waltzes of Rodolphe Berger instead of my scales. St Cecilia lay smiling on a couch with one finger over three to symbolize that she believed in the Three in One.

So the tableaux went on and we peeped at the bishop, but he didn't applaud. The old bishop always clapped loudly and smiled, but this bishop seemed very bored.

When the programme ended we trooped onto the stage to hear the bishop give his little speech of thanks and appreciation. There was a pause, because for some reason he didn't seem able to get up. He put his hands on the arms of the chair, turned round, glared and tried again. No use.

Soon it was plain what had happened; he had stuck to the chair, which had been taken to be varnished and the varnish hadn't quite dried. Some of the nuns looked apprehensive and hurried to help him, but Mother Superior, who dearly loved a joke, couldn't stop herself from smiling broadly.. Just as she smiled the bishop looked straight at her, their eyes met, she suppressed the smile, but it was too late.

Soon afterwards he came to the school to give us dictation. I liked the colour of his purple skull cap but I hated his face. The old bishop had a light voice, he had a heavy throaty voice. He dictated: 'I have a dog. His name is Toby. He can bark and he can bite….'

That's how it began. He started trying to get rid of them even before I left the island.

Of course Mother Mount Calvary had her friends and must have fought back, but even she couldn't fight old age. It was a sad meeting. When I left them I promised to visit them again before they sailed.

But I never saw them again. I went away to spend a week on the Atlantic side of the island, and when I returned to the town the day before they were to leave, I was told that Mother Mount Calvary had died that morning. I felt very sad, but also something like triumph, because in the end she had won. She had always done what she said she'd do. She had said she would never leave the island, and she hadn't.

Temps Perdi

'Rolvenden' is a square, red-brick house, and it stands with two others on the farthest outskirts of a good-sized village on the east coast. It belongs to one of the masters of a small public school which has moved to Gloucestershire for safety's sake. There is nothing in the house that you can say is ugly; on the other hand there is nothing that you can say is beautiful, impulsive, impetuous or generous. All is sparse, subdued, quiet and negative, or so you would think – a lawn, a large vegetable garden, an empty garage and, when I first came, a few last sad flowers. Outside the front door a gravel path, once bordered with lavender, leads to a green gate.

The two other houses have been taken over by the Army. The one opposite has large grounds and I never hear a sound from it. But from the one on the side there is often the clatter of men washing up ill-temperedly. How they chuck the things about! This is the time of smash and grab. Some poor devil – or rich devil or stupid devil – had tried hard with that house. There are four bathrooms – pink, black, green and blue. But there is venom in the way those men wash up, and there won't be much left of the pink, black, green and blue bathrooms when the military have got out.

But why be glad? Above all, why be sad? Death brings its own anaesthetic, or so they say....

Behind the garden wall there is land and a row of cottages. Never a sound from them either. At first I thought there wasn't a living soul there, but I learnt better later.

In justice to 'Rolvenden' I must say that it has changed a great deal since I have lived in it, and in fairness to myself I must add that I knew at once that we shouldn't get on and argued that I did not want to live there alone – especially in

October, November, December and January. But there are
times when one is helpless. However, only the helpless know
this – and why preach to the converted?

A few days ago, or a week ago – I have forgotten – it began to
snow. Since then I have been quite happy. Yes, since the snow
started falling I have been much happier, though I don't
trouble to look at it. Why look at it when I remember so well the
first time I saw it? It was better then – it was a marvel, the only
thing in England that hadn't disappointed me. (Remembering
when I used to have to touch and taste it every time it fell....)

Now, on my way to the garage in the morning to bring in
coal, I see the black trunks of the trees in the garden and the
thin, pointing branches, then hurry in to light the fire and
make my bacon sandwich and cup of coffee essence. After that
I can lie for a long time watching the neutral sitting-room and
the rows of extraordinary books without being angry or afraid
or hoping. Now I am almost as wary of books as I am of people.
They also are capable of hurting you, pushing you into the
limbo of the forgotten. They can tell lies – and vulgar, trivial
lies – and when there are so many all saying the same thing
they can shout you down and make you doubt, not only your
memory, but your senses. However, I have discovered one or
two of the opposition. Listen: '...to conduct the transposition
of the souls of the dead to the White Island, in the manner just
described. The White Island is occasionally also called Brea, or
Britannia. Does this perhaps refer to White Albion, to the
chalky cliffs of the English coast? It would be a very humorous
idea if England was designated as the land of the dead...as
hell. In such a form, in truth, England has appeared to many a
stranger.' (To many a stranger....)

Also I have discovered how to keep warm. You drape a
blanket over the door, which stops the draught from the
keyhole and the cracks, and a bolster finishes it off. And now I
know how to pile the cushions so that I can sit on the floor in
front of the fire without slipping backwards. The solid,
uncomfortable chairs help. I am learning how to make use of
you, my enemy.

The piano is out of tune. It gives a cracked, shattered and
ghostly sound, it complains like a hurt animal when I play

'Mama, I want to make rhythm, I want to make music' and 'Time on my hands', then backwards to 'Si j'avais su – évidemment', backwards again to the waltz of Nina Rodriguez, never forgotten, heard so long ago.

Said to be twelve, Nina was probably sixteen or seventeen. She was a performer in a Havana circus which was touring the smaller Caribbean islands. It was the first theatrical performance I had ever seen. The circus tent was as huge as a cathedral to me, and the trapeze impossibly high and frail. It was lighted by glaring acetylene lamps.

The Rodriguez family were the stars. Mr Rodriguez, burly and sinister, always wore light-blue tights; Madame Rodriguez, pale, sad and mournful under her make-up wore pink or red, and lovely Nina – the Only Girl Who Works Without a Net – wore black. Black tights to match her black eyes. And her golden curls were hanging down her back, too. We craned our necks to watch her, a black and gold butterfly caught in a web, weaving in and out of the web, miraculously escaping, miraculously coming to earth again, giving the two little stylized hops, smiling, kissing her hands to us.

Pale Madame Rodriguez worked on a higher trapeze. The net was brought in with much ceremony and there was a big roll of drums for the dangerous bit, but it wasn't the same thing and I don't remember a note of her waltz.

I was in the kitchen making a bacon sandwich when the coal arrived. It had been worrying me – there was so little left in the garage and all the coal in the bin outside the kitchen had disappeared. The people from the cottages in the lane took most of it – at first surreptitiously when I was out; after they had sized me up, openly.

The clatter of coal on zinc. Then a man's voice said, 'That's the bathroom.'

'Well what about it? Why are you looking at it? Is there a woman in the ditch?' said a second voice.

'Why d'you think I'd look at her if there was?' the first voice said, very offended. 'Why should you think I'd look at a blank, blank cow in a blank, blank, blank ditch?'

I walked out of the kitchen and scowled at them. These people are altogether too much.... They jeered back at me.

'You shouldn't have put the coal in that bin,' I said in an old shrew's voice. 'You should have asked me. You should have put it in the garage. Every lump of it will get stolen there. It was full when I came and it's all gone now because there are a lot of thieves round here, and mean thieves too. There are meaner thieves here than anywhere I've ever been in my life.'

'A-ah?' said the one of them.

'It ought to have a padlock on it,' the second one said, helpfully: 'What can you expect if it hasn't got a padlock on it?'

They both wear the local mask – beige in colour as usual.

'Go to hell,' I said.

The first man answered gently, 'Yes, it's very cold today, isn't it, Miss?'

The second one said, 'Very cold weather, Madam,' he said, winking at the first one.

They went off and I started after them. They must be frozen. Shall I call to them and ask them in to have some coffee essence? They might warm the place.

But before they got to the garden gate – 'Rolvenden' is painted on it – I saw that they were shaking with laughter. Silent, smothered laughter – never, even with them, a good, hearty shout or curse, just this silent, sly, shy laughter. I can imagine what they would have said about me if I had asked them indoors.

That's an exaggeration. They don't think or say anything that I would imagine they would think or say. Speak for yourself and no falsities. There are enough falsities; enough harm has been done.

For all that was left of the afternoon I carried scuttles of coal from the bin outside the kitchen to the garage, which can be locked, and the house watched me haughtily, seeing me as I really am. And once or twice I looked back at it and thought that maybe I too saw it as it really was. But it will certainly defeat me, for it has one great quality – it is very cunning. It knows how to hide its hate under a hypocrite's mask – again a beige mask, of course – for all here is beige that can be beige, paint, carpets, curtains, upholstery, bedspreads. Everything wears this neutral mask – the village, the people, the sky, even the trees have not escaped.

But before I had half-emptied the bin I felt as tired as if I had walked fifty miles – tired and in utter despair. This bath will always be a ditch to me now and a dirty ditch at that. I was too tired to eat but went up to bed with a beer-bottle filled with hot water to keep me warm.

All the beds are cold, narrow and hard. There are three bedrooms. Photographs of Greek temples – I suppose they are temples, pillars anyway – decorate the walls of this one. There is a cheap dressing-table with a glass that won't stay put, a wardrobe to match the dressing-table and a straight-backed chair. Here too I have put bolsters along the window-sills, because I remember how well they kept out the cold in Vienna. Slowly I grow calmer, and then quite calm. I know that the second stage of loneliness is over and the bad moment is past.

Looking at the bolsters and remembering the piles of yellow-white snow and that statue of the Holy Ghost. 'Clouds in stone,' said André. 'Very German! Like the insides of a turkey.' Another time he said 'The legs are the most noble, beautiful, harmonious and interesting part of the human body.' I said No, I didn't agree. We argued sitting at a table in the *Parisien* with bottles of German champagne before us. But it was not chic to drink it. Now and again you foamed up your glass with one of those wooden instruments they had and then pretended to sip. I can see us sitting there and I can see my astrakhan coat and the dress I was wearing, but it is not myself inside it. Everything is sharp, bright, clear-cut – a little smaller than life, perhaps, and the voices coming from some way off, but very clear. It is 'Rolvenden' that is behind me in the mist.

In the bedroom of the flat in the Razumoffskygasse there were low coffee tables, Bohemian glass, a big picture of Franz Josef and smaller pictures on either side of General and Madame von Marken. Pierre came in and said 'Bravo' when he saw me in my new black dress. There was a smell of lilac when you got out into the street, of lilac, of drains and of the past. Yes, that's what Vienna smelt of then....

2 *The Sword Dance and the Love Dance*

Every fortnight the officers of the Japanese Commission entertained their following at Sacher's Hotel. The Japanese were very dependent on their following, for not one of them could speak all three of the necessary languages – French,

English, German. There were perpetual arguments over the exact translation of documents. They were afraid of not being as tactful as the representatives of an Asiatic power ought to be, or of voting with the minority instead of the majority – that would have been the end of them in Tokyo. So Colonel Hato had his secretary and confidential adviser – that was André – and Lieutenant-Colonel Matsu had his – that was Pierre. Then there were four other officers (at first – the number increased by leaps and bounds later on), a naval attaché, the typists, who had been carefully chosen by Matsu in Paris and were all very easy on the eye though by no means all of them were efficient according to Pierre, a Hungarian interpreter, and various other hangers-on.

At the end of the long, elaborate meal some of the guests would leave and the rest of us would go into Matsu's sitting-room next door – high, silk-curtained windows, gilt furniture, shining mirrors. Then bottles of Tokay and kümmel appeared and the Japanese mask dropped. Then photographs would be produced and handed round.

'This is Madame Yoshi.'

'How pretty she is!'

'She's wearing European clothes.'

'Oh, doesn't she look smiling and happy?'

'Of course she is smiling,' Captain Yoshi said – rather grimly, I thought – 'Madame Yoshi is a most fortunate woman. Madame Yoshi *knows* that she is a most fortunate woman.'

Matsu's photographs were of his little son and of his three daughters, whose names meant Early Rising, Order and Morning Sun. He had bought them each a typewriter as a present. He never told us the son's name, or what present was destined for him. Too sacred?

Captain Oyazu had no photographs, but in next to no time he could transform the evening paper into a frog which looked as if it might start hopping at any moment, and he smiled in a pleased, childlike way when you admired it.

On this particular evening Colonel Hato and Oyazu left after the first glass of Tokay, and as soon as they had gone Yoshi began to dance.

Yoshi was the tallest, handsomest and best-dressed of the Japanese officers and he spoke French and German better than any of the others. First he danced the sword dance, using umbrellas instead of swords, and then what I suppose was a love dance, for, turning his feet out at right angles and holding an umbrella upright, he shuffled past us, looking at the women of the party very slanting-eyed and mocking.

But Simone, who was the prettiest of the typists and only eighteen years of age, answered that challenge at once. She danced opposite him with her hands on her hips, laughing, imitating exactly every step he made, and after a bit of this the strain and defiance went out of his face. He pulled her to him and began a clumsy foxtrot. André played 'Dardanella' for them on the piano.

When 'Dardanella' was finished Matsu announced, 'I will now play you a Japanese song.'

He played it with one finger, striking the notes carefully and gently, with a sad, absorbed, intent expression.

He said – he was the one who spoke English – 'That is a sleep song.'

Matsu had spent a fortnight in London and for a whole day of it he had been lost in the Inner Circle. 'When I came out it was very dark and cold. I grew frightened and sad.' (He was in London in November.)

After the lullaby he went off into a long, monotonous succession of notes, as if he were trying to make a pattern of the keys, black and white. There was music in him somewhere – he touched the piano so gently.

Yoshi and Simone were sitting at a table at the far end of the room. The others were gossiping about Hato. There was always a new story going about him. He was the one who loathed white people and said so, maintaining that contact with them would bring nothing but misfortune to Japan. He was the one who, safe in his bedroom, André said, would at once take off his European clothes, saying that they made him feel unclean, and put on a kimono and slippers with hisses of relief.

He was a small, thin man, much older than any of the others. Really very old, we thought, quite gaga. He had only one eye – he had lost the other in the Russo-Japanese War, and it had not been dolled up, either. On social occasions he would sit bolt upright, silent, staring into the distance.

'What can he be thinking of, André?'

André said, 'The poor devil is supposed to speak French. And he can't. I should say that gives him enough to think about.'

But he, too, liked music. His favourite song was 'Marjolaine'. 'Encore "Marjolaine",' he would shout. (Si gracile, si fragile…) 'Encore, encore "Marjolaine".'

When they had finished with Hato, Odette, another of the typists, began to tell us what she thought about Viennese clothes. She said that they were pretty but they had no real chic. 'When I went back to Paris on leave last month Maman told me, "You look like a little provincial". Maman is thirty-nine but one would say twenty-five. She cried like a Magdalene when I left –'

André interrupted, 'My God, what's happening over there?'

Yoshi was sprawled on the floor, the table and the bottle of wine were upset. He got up and brushed his clothes down, though without smiling or looking at us. André rushed forward and picked up the table and the bottle. Simone said, 'Oh, do excuse me. I'm such a clumsy girl. I've always been like that. You've no idea – the trouble I get into because –'

Soon afterwards we said good night and were out in the lilac-scented street. After we got round the first corner Simone began to laugh. She had held it in like a good one, but now it had to come out.

'How did it happen, Simone?' André said at last.

Simone said, 'I don't know how it happened. He was practising kissing the hand and I'd had enough of it and tried to pull away. He held on and crashed into the table, and down he went. I expect he'd had too much to drink. Oh, his face when he fell! Aren't they funny? And those dances with the umbrellas!'

Off she went again.

Pierre said, 'I hope he won't bear you any malice, Simone. I'd hate to be somebody the Japanese bore malice against.'

'Not he,' Simone said. 'He won't bear any malice against me, poor boy.'

None of us thought of taking cabs home that night. Perhaps

there was a moon. Perhaps the streets were lovelier or more deserted than usual. Then there was that smell of lilac and of the past. Vienna still smelt very strongly of the past. We walked along, keeping rather close together.

'Well,' I said, 'he looked as if he were telling you all his secrets.'

'He was,' Simone said, 'he was. Do you know what he was saying? He was saying how much he admires the Germans. He said they'll soon have the best army in Europe, and that they'll dominate it in a few years.'

'No bouquet for the French?' André asked, laughing 'And think how I sweat, translating their idiotic ideas into diplomatic language!'

Simone answered seriously, 'But he did say something about the French. He said the French love women too much. He said only the Germans know how to treat women. The Germans and the English think the same way about women, he said, but the French think differently. He said the English and the French together won't last another year, and that they are splitting up already.'

Pierre said, 'Oh, he's found that out, has he? Not much they don't find out.'

We walked on.

Odette said in a sullen voice, 'I'm not Anglophile, me. And why do all their songs sound like hymns?'

'I like them,' Simone said happily. 'Oh, I like some of those boys. Their clothes are so chic and they can be very nice. I like them. I like everything – everybody.' She spread her arms wide open.

'And then you wake up,' I thought.

'What beautiful enthusiasm, Simone!' said André.

Odette said, 'It's true that the English have droll ideas. The other day I was talking to Captain – You know the one, the one with the long nose and the monocle. And he said, "I've just seen an amazingly pretty woman –" Then he stopped and went as red as fire. So out of spite I pretended I hadn't heard; I made him repeat it. "I've just seen rather an attractive *person*," he said, "in the Kärntnerstrasse." Why should he have to blush like that, when he says the word woman? Is it a dirty word in English?'

'Because he's an idiot,' Pierre said, 'and so are you a little idiot, Odette.'

'All the same,' André said, 'there's something in it. "Ma femme," you say; "Meine Frau," you say. But what would happen if you said "May I introduce my woman, Mrs Colonel?"'

'It depends on Mrs Colonel, but I shouldn't risk it,' I said.

'I used to mix up the words myself when I first learnt English,' André remarked. 'That's how I know the difference is very important. Also there's lady and girl. Very complicated.'

Of course we all knew that there were a lot of sly jokes, misunderstandings, cartoons and so on, about the British in Vienna. It was not altogether their fault – they were severely handicapped. Love affairs with Viennese girls were very much discouraged, so when they occurred they were carried on cautiously and often ended brutally. On the other hand, 'great friendships' with boys were winked at – even with the boys who at one café were to be found heavily made up and dressed in women's evening clothes. But everybody said that you ought to see them in Berlin; Vienna wasn't their home town.

André said, 'I bet if they knew in Tokyo what Yoshi told Simone there'd be trouble. They're not orthodox, these confidences.'

'No need for Tokyo,' Pierre said 'You've only got to tell Hato. Then Yoshi would have to commit hara-kiri. Hato detests him.'

'Wouldn't that be a feather in Hato's cap?' I said.

And we all knew that not one of us would stick that feather in Hato's cap. He hated us, so we hated him – it's easy.

We had nearly reached the hotel where the girls were staying.

'Did he really say that, Simone,' asked André, 'about the English and the French splitting up, and the next war?'

'He did, I assure you,' said Simone, 'he did. He said he gave it ten to fifteen years, and after that Germany would probably dominate Europe. He said it would happen because the English and the French don't trust each other and can't stick together and that's the only thing that might stop it.'

'Ten to fifteen years is a long time,' Odette said.

'And Japan?' said Pierre. 'And beautiful Nippon? Banzai Nippon!'

'He didn't say anything about Japan,' said Simone, 'now I come to think of it. Not a word about Nippon.'

We said good night to the girls. We didn't talk for a bit. Then André said. 'The Japanese! They are not to be taken seriously. What can they possibly know about it?'

Yes, I can remember all my dresses, except the one on the chair beside me, the one I wore when I was walking on the cliffs yesterday. Yesterday – when was yesterday?...

I had a striped taffeta dress, with velvet flowers tucked into the tight waistband. (And the waistband was round the waist, whatever the English fashion was then.) I had a white satin dress, very slick and smooth, the prettiest of the lot but the cheapest. Round the throat there were coloured stones imitating a necklace. I had a black satin dress with three flounces bordered with green, hand-sewn. With this dress I had two sashes to wear, each as elaborate as a Japanese *obi*. One was black, boned so that it made my waist look very small; the other was green, to match the borders of the flounces. I had a white muslin dress that washed like a rag, and a blue one too, made just the same. Those were my favourites. Washed and ironed like rags, they did, and always came up as fresh as daisies. I had a dirndl, and a check dress. I had a blue serge dress, the bodice fitting closely but the skirt wide and full. Its sleeves were loose, embroidered in gay colours and finished with a tassel. I had a classic English *tailleur*, but I always hated that. I had a yellow and blue dress to wear when I wanted to lie down, when I was tired. It was long and loose, the neck and sleeves bordered with blue. It was like cornfields and the sky, and looking at it made you feel happy, made you feel free. And thinking of it I am free again, knowing that nobody can stop me thinking, thinking of my dresses, of mirrors and pictures, of stones and clouds and mountains and the days that wait for you round the corner to be lived again. Riding round and round the Inner Circle, but unlike Matsu I ride knowing that it will be dark and cold when I come out, that it will be November, and that I shall be a savage person – a real Carib.

But Caribs live under different skies, by a different sea. 'They run and hide when they see anybody,' Nicholas said. Perhaps I shall do that too.

3 *Carib Quarter*

Nicholas was the overseer of Temps Perdi, an estate near the Carib Quarter. Temps Perdi is Creole patois and does not mean, poetically, lost or forgotten time, but, matter-of-factly wasted time, lost labour. There are places which are supposed to be hostile to human beings and to know how to defend themselves. When I was a child it used to be said that this island was one of them. You are getting along fine and then a hurricane comes, or a disease of the crops that nobody can cure, and there you are – more West Indian ruins and labour lost. It has been going on for more than three hundred years – yes, it's more than three hundred years ago that somebody carved 'Temps Perdi' on a tree near by, they say.

The estate house had been empty for so long that a centipede fell out of a book when I opened it. Everything had run wild, but there was still hibiscus growing by the stone garden walls and butterflies made love over the thorny bougainvillea. Every morning Myra, Nicholas's daughter, put little earthenware bowls of fresh flowers along the low partition which separated the verandah from the sitting-room. From the verandah we could see Guadeloupe, the Saints and Marie Galante; sun on dark trees....

But the white-cedars at the end of the garden – the lowest about eight feet high – had dropped their leaves and were covered with flowers, white flowers very faintly tinged with pink, so light and fragile that they fell with the first high wind and were blown away as soon as they fell. There used to be a famous Creole song about the white-cedar flowers but I can't remember it. 'Here today and gone tomorrow' – something like that, it must be.

'There is nothing to see in the Carib Quarter,' Nicholas insisted. He had a handsome negro face, a big chest, a deep, booming voice.

'These people,' he said, 'don't even live near together. Their houses are each far away from the other, and all hidden in the bush. There is nothing to see in Salybia. Besides, the new road only goes as far as the river. After that you'll have to ride. It will take a couple of hours or so.'

'But can't it be arranged? Can't we get the horses?'

'Oh yes, it can be arranged,' Nicholas said disapprovingly.

But I wasn't so easily put off. All my life I had been curious about these people because of a book I once read, pictures I once saw.

Whenever the Caribs are talked about, which is not often, the adjective is 'decadent', though nobody knows much about them, one way or the other, or ever will now. There are only a few hundreds left in the West Indies, or in the world, and they live in the part of this island called Salybia. They have not intermarried much with the negroes and still have smooth, black hair, small, slanting eyes, high cheekbones, copper-coloured skins. They make baskets, beautifully plaited, light and waterproof, dyed red and brown or black and white. The largest is the island's substitute for a trunk, the smallest would just hold a baby's shoe. Sometimes the baskets are made to fit one inside the other, like Chinese boxes.

Nobody else seemed to want to visit the Carib Quarter, nobody seemed at all anxious to take a long ride in the sun with nothing much to see at the end of it.

'They are supposed to have two languages. The women have a language that the men don't know. So they say.'

'They say so, do they?'

'Well, we'll ask Nicholas…. Nicholas, isn't it true that the Carib women have a secret language?'

Nicholas said, grinning, that he thought he had heard something of the sort. Yes, he fancied he had.

Tormented with the fear that I had imagined the closely-printed book, the gaudy illustrations pored over as a child, I produced the special number of *L'Illustration*, 23 November 1935, for the *Tricentenaire des Antilles Françaises* and exhibited *'Homme Caraibe Dessiné d'après natur par le Père Plumier'*. Early eighteenth century, probably. Bow and arrows in his right hand, a club in his left, a huge, muscular body and a strange, small, womanish face. His long, black hair was carefully parted in the middle and hung smoothly to his shoulders. But his slanting eyes, starting from their sockets, looked wild and terrified. He was more the frightened than the frightening savage.

'We had a print very like this – perhaps it was the same one – in the dining-room at home.'

'He isn't very attractive.'

'Everybody used to say that.'

And he always used to look so sad, I thought, when they laughed at him. With his wild, strained eyes and his useless bows and arrows.

'The original West Indian, is he?'

'Oh no, that's a Carib. The original West Indians were killed by the Spaniards or deported to Hispaniola – Haiti. Well, most of the men were. The Spaniards told them they were going to Heaven. So they went. Weren't they suckers? Then the Caribs, the cannibals, came from the mainland of South America and killed off the few men who were left.'

But that book, written by an Englishman in the 1880s, said that some of the women, who had survived both Spaniards and Caribs – people were not so thorough then as they are now – had carried on the old language and traditions, handing them down from mother to daughter. This language was kept a secret from their conquerors, but the writer of the book claimed to have learned it. He said that it was Mongolian in origin, not South American. He said that it definitely established the fact that there was communication between China and what is now known as the New World. But he had a lot of imagination, that man. Wasn't there a chapter about the buried Carib treasure in La Soufrière, St Lucia – one of the mouths of Hell, they say – and another about the snake god, and another about Atlantis? Oh yes, he had a lot of imagination.

The day we went to the Carib Quarter the wind was blowing heavy luminous clouds across the sky, tormenting the thin crooked coconut-palms on the slope of the hill opposite the verandah, so different from the straight, healthy, glossy-green coconuts just round the corner of the road – tame trees, planted in rows to make copra. We arrived punctually at the place where the horses were to wait for us, but it was a long wait before they turned up, so young Charlie, aged sixteen, who was our guide, went on ahead. He was beautifully got up in white shirt, shorts and socks, but hideous, heavy black boots that squeaked with every step he took. There were stepping-stones across the shallowest part of the broad river. On one of these Charlie's horrible boots betrayed him and I thought he had fallen into the water, but he managed to save himself. When he got to the other side it was a relief to see him sit down, take off his boots and socks and hang them round his neck before he walked on.

The horses came at last. They were so thin that every bone showed in their bodies and they had the morose, obstinate expression which is the price of survival in hostile surroundings. Negroes like to be in the movement and hate anything old-fashioned, and horses are now definitely old-fashioned.

However, when we mounted they jerked their necks strongly and clip-clopped without hesitation into the clear, shallow river. I had forgotten the lovely sound of horses' hooves in water, that I hadn't heard for so many damnable years.

Then they heaved and strained us on to a wide, grassy road. There was a flamboyant tree with a few flowers out. Next month, I thought, it will be covered; next month all the flamboyant trees – the flame trees – will be covered, and the immortelles will flower, but I shan't be here to see them. I'll be on my way back to England then, I thought, and felt giddy and sick. There were a lot of iguanas along that road. I shut my eyes and saw one of the illustrations in the book about the Caribs, vivid, complete in every detail. A brown girl, crowned with flowers, a parrot on her shoulder, welcoming the Spaniards, the long-prophesied gods. Behind her the rest of the population crowded, carrying presents of fruit and flowers, but some of them very scowling and suspicious – and how right they were!

In the midst of this dream, riding through a desolate, arid, lizard-ridden country, different and set apart from the island I knew, I was still sensitive to the opinion of strangers and dreaded hostile criticism. But no, it was approved of, more or less. 'Beautiful, open, park-like country. But what an *extreme* green!'

The road had been gradually rising and, as we came round the shoulder of a hill, smiling Charlie met us, accompanied by a negro policeman. An official welcome to Salybia?... Below us we saw small clearings among the low trees – low for that part of the world – and the bush riddled with narrow paths. But not a human being. ('These people live all separated from each other, and all hidden in the bush. These people hide when they see anybody.')

'That's the king's house,' the policeman announced, and I thought 'So, there's still a king, is there?'

Round another bend in the road we saw below us the big clearing where the police-station stood with five or six other houses, one of them a Catholic church.

In the station the rifles were stacked in a row, bayonets and all. The room was large, almost cool. Everything looked new and clean, and there was a circular seat round the palm tree outside.

'We had trouble here,' our policeman told us. 'They burnt the last station and they burnt twenty feet off this one while it was being built.'

'Why?'

'Well, it seems they thought they were going to have a hospital. They had asked the Government for a hospital. A petition, you know. And when they found out that the Government was giving them a police-station and not a hospital, there was trouble.'

'Serious trouble?'

'Pretty serious. They burnt the first one down, and they burnt twenty feet off this one.'

'Yes, but I mean was anybody hurt?'

'Oh no, only two or three Caribs,' he said. 'Two-three Caribs were killed.' It might have been an Englishman talking.

'There is a beautiful Carib girl,' the policeman said, 'in the house over there – the one with the red roof. Everybody goes to see her and photographs her. She and her mother will be vexed if you don't go. Give her a little present, of course. She is very beautiful but she can't walk. It's a pity, that.'

When you went in it was like all their houses. A small room, clean, the walls covered with pictures cut from newspapers

and coloured cards of Virgins, saints and angels, Star of the
Sea, Refuge of the Distressed, Hope of the Afflicted, Star of the
Sea again, Jesus, Mary and Joseph....

The girl appeared in the doorway of the dark little bedroom,
posed for a moment dramatically, then dragged herself across
the floor into the sun outside to be photographed, managing
her useless legs with a desperate, courageous grace; she had
white, lovely teeth. There she sat in the sun, brown eyes fixed
on us, the long brown eyes of the Creole, not the small, black,
slanting eyes of the pure Carib. And her hair, which hung to
her waist and went through every shade from dark brown to
copper and back again, was not a Carib's hair, either. She sat
there smiling, and an assortment of brightly-coloured Virgins
and saints looked down at her from the walls, smiling too. She
had aquiline features, proud features. Her skin in the sun was
a lovely colour.

We took a few photographs, then Charlie asked if he might
take the rest. We heard his condescending voice: 'Will you
turn your side face? Will you please turn your full face? *Don't*
smile for this one.' ('These people are quite savage people –
quite uncivilized.')

Her mother, who looked like an old Chinese woman, told us
that in her youth she had lived in Martinique in service with a
French family and then had been taken to Paris.

'I come back here,' she said, 'because I want to see my
mother before she die. I loved my mother. Now I must stay
because I am old, I am old and who will take me away?'

'She like that since she four,' she said, pointing to her
daugher.

'Hélas!' she said, gesticulating. She had thin, lovely hands.
'Hélas, hélas!'

But the girl, sitting in the sun to be photographed, smiled
contentedly at us, pushed a strand of hair from her shoulder to
her back, smiled again. And all the Virgins and saints on the
walls smiled at us too.

The night in Temps Perdi is full of things chirping and
fluttering. The fireflies are out – they call them labelles. It is at
night, lying caged under a mosquito-net, that you think, 'Now
I am home, where the earth is sometimes red and sometimes

black. Round about here it is ochre – a Carib skin. In some lights like blood, in others just pretty, like a picture postcard coloured by somebody with a child's paintbox and no imagination.'

It is at night that you know old fears, old hopes, that you know unhappiness, turning from side to side under the mosquito-net, like a prisoner in a cell full of small peepholes. Then you think of that plant with thick, fleshy leaves edged with thorns, on which some up-to-the-minute negro has written over and over again 'Girls muck, girls muck', and other monosyllabic and elementary truths. When I was a child we used to draw hearts pierced with arrows on leaves like that and 'Z loves A'. It all comes to the same thing, probably.

But when you have drunk a good tot of rum nothing dismays you; you know the password and the Open Sesame. You drink a second; then you understand everything – the sun, the flamboyance, the girl crawling (because she could not walk) across the floor to be photographed. And the song about the white-cedar trees. 'Ma belle ka di maman-li–' (A lot of their songs begin like that – 'My lovely girl said to her mother.') 'Why do the flowers last only a day?' the girl says. 'It's very sad. Why?' The mother says 'One day and a thousand years are the same for the Bon Dieu.' I wish I could remember it all but it is useless trying to find out because nobody sings these old songs any more.

It had a sweet sound sometimes, patois. And I can't get the words out of my mind, Temps Perdi.

Before I leave 'Rolvenden' I'll write them up – on a looking glass, perhaps. Somebody might see them who knows about the days that wait round the corner to be lived again and knows that you don't choose them, either. They choose themselves.

I Used to Live Here Once

She was standing by the river looking at the stepping stones and remembering each one. There was the round unsteady stone, the pointed one, the flat one in the middle –the safe stone where you could stand and look round. The next wasn't so safe for when the river was full the water flowed over it and even when it showed dry it was slippery. But after that it was easy and soon she was standing on the other side.

The road was much wider that it used to be but the work had been done carelessly. The felled trees had not been cleared away and the bushes looked trampled. Yet it was the same road and she walked along feeling extraordinarily happy.

It was a fine day, a blue day. The only thing was that the sky had a glassy look that she didn't remember. That was the only word she could think of. Glassy. She turned the corner, saw that what had been the old pavé had been taken up, and there too the road was much wider, but it had the same unfinished look.

She came to the worn stone steps that led up to the house and her heart began to beat. The screw pine was gone, so was the mock summer house called the ajoupa, but the clove tree was still there and at the top of the steps the rough lawn stretched away, just as she remembered it. She stopped and looked towards the house that had been added to and painted white. It was strange to see a car standing in front of it.

There were two children under the big mango tree, a boy and a little girl, and she waved to them and called 'Hello' but they didn't answer her or turn their heads. Very fair children, as Europeans born in the West Indies so often are: as if the white blood is asserting itself against all odds.

The grass was yellow in the hot sunlight as she walked

towards them. When she was quite close she called again, shyly: 'Hello.' Then, 'I used to live here once,' she said.

Still they didn't answer. When she said for the third time 'Hello' she was quite near them. Her arms went out instinctively with the longing to touch them.

It was the boy who turned. His grey eyes looked straight into hers. His expression didn't change. He said: 'Hasn't it gone cold all of a sudden. D'you notice? Let's go in.' 'Yes let's,' said the girl.

Her arms fell to her sides as she watched them running across the grass to the house. That was the first time she knew.

Let Them Call it Jazz

One bright Sunday morning in July I have trouble with my Notting Hill landlord because he ask for a month's rent in advance. He tell me this after I live there since winter, settling up every week without fail. I have no job at the time, and if I give the money he want there's not much left. So I refuse. The man drunk already at that early hour, and he abuse me – all talk, he can't frighten me. But his wife is a bad one – now she walk in my room and say she must have cash. When I tell her no, she give my suitcase one kick and it burst open. My best dress fall out, then she laugh and give another kick. She say month in advance is usual, and if I can't pay find somewhere else.

Don't talk to me about London. Plenty people there have heart like stone. Any complaint – the answer is 'prove it'. But if nobody see and bear witness for me, how to prove anything? So I pack up and leave, I think better not have dealings with that woman. She too cunning, and Satan don't lie worse.

I walk about till a place nearby is open where I can have coffee and a sandwich. There I start talking to a man at my table. He talk to me already, I know him, but I don't know his name. After a while he ask, 'What's the matter? Anything wrong?' and when I tell him my trouble he say I can use an empty flat he own till I have time to look around.

This man is not at all like most English people. He see very quick, and he decide very quick. English people take long time to decide – you three-quarter dead before they make up their mind about you. Too besides, he speak very matter of fact, as if it's nothing. He speak as if he realize well what it is to live like I do – that's why I accept and go.

He tell me somebody occupy the flat till last week, so I find everything all right, and he tell me how to get there – three-quarters of an hour from Victoria Station, up a steep hill, turn left, and I can't mistake the house. He give me the keys and an envelope with a telephone number on the back. Underneath is written 'After 6 p.m. ask for Mr Sims'.

In the train that evening I think myself lucky, for to walk about London on a Sunday with nowhere to go – that take the heart out of you.

I find the place and the bedroom of the downstairs flat is nicely furnished – two looking glass, wardrobe, chest of drawers, sheets, everything. It smell of jasmine scent, but it smell strong of damp too.

I open the door opposite and there's a table, a couple chairs, a gas stove and a cupboard, but this room so big it look empty. When I pull the blind up I notice the paper peeling off and mushrooms growing on the walls – you never see such a thing.

The bathroom the same, all the taps rusty. I leave the two other rooms and make up the bed. Then I listen, but I can't hear one sound. Nobody come in, nobody go out of that house. I lie awake for a long time, then I decide not to stay and in the morning I start to get ready quickly before I change my mind. I want to wear my best dress, but it's a funny thing – when I take up that dress and remember how my landlady kick it I cry. I cry and I can't stop. When I stop I feel tired to my bones, tired like old woman. I don't want to move again – I have to force myself. But in the end I get out in the passage and there's a postcard for me. 'Stay as long as you like. I'll be seeing you soon – Friday probably. Not to worry.' It isn't signed, but I don't feel so sad and I think, 'All right, I wait here till he come. Perhaps he know of a job for me.'

Nobody else live in the house but a couple on the top floor – quiet people and they don't trouble me. I have no word to say against them.

First time I meet the lady she's opening the front door and she give me a very inquisitive look. But the next time she smile a bit and I smile back – once she talk to me. She tell me the house very old, hundred and fifty year old, and she and her husband live there since long time. 'Valuable property,' she says, 'it could have been saved, but nothing done of course.' Then she tells me that as to the present owner – if he is the owner – well he have to deal with local authorities and she believe they make difficulties. 'These people are determined to pull down all the lovely old houses – it's shameful.'

So I agree that many things shameful. But what to do? What to do? I say it have an elegant shape, it make the other houses in the street look cheap trash, and she seem pleased. That's true too. The house sad and out of place, especially at night. But it have style. The second floor shut up, and as for my flat, I go in the two empty rooms once, but never again.

Underneath was the cellar, full of old boards and broken-up furniture – I see a big rat there one day. It was no place to be alone in I tell you, and I get the habit of buying a bottle of wine most evenings, for I don't like whisky and the rum here no good. It don't even *taste* like rum. You wonder what they do to it.

After I drink a glass or two I can sing and when I sing all the misery goes from my heart. Sometimes I make up songs but next morning I forget them, so other times I sing the old ones like *Tantalizin'* or *Don't Trouble Me Now*.

I think I go but I don't go. Instead I wait for the evening and the wine and that's all. Everywhere else I live – well, it doesn't matter to me, but this house is different – empty and no noise and full of shadows, so that sometimes you ask yourself what make all those shadows in an empty room.

I eat in the kitchen, then I clean up everything nice and have a bath for coolness. Afterwards I lean my elbows on the windowsill and look at the garden. Red and blue flowers mix up with the weeds and there are five-six apple trees. But the fruit drop and lie in the grass, so sour nobody want it. At the back, near the wall, is a bigger tree – this garden certainly take up a lot of room, perhaps that's why they want to pull the place down.

Not much rain all the summer, but not much sunshine either. More of a glare. The grass get brown and dry, the weeds grow tall, the leaves on the trees hang down. Only the red flowers – the poppies – stand up to that light, everything else look weary.

I don't trouble about money, but what with wine and shillings for the slot-meters, it go quickly; so I don't waste much on food. In the evening I walk outside – not by the apple trees but near the street – it's not so lonely.

There's no wall here and I can see the woman next door looking at me over the hedge. At first I say good evening, but she turn away her head, so afterwards I don't speak. A man is often with her, he wear a straw hat with a black ribbon and goldrim spectacles. His suit hang on him like it's too big. He's the husband it seems and he stare at me worse than his wife – he stare as if I'm wild animal let loose. Once I laugh in his face because why these people have to be like that? I don't bother them. In the end I get that I don't even give them one single glance. I have plenty other things to worry about.

To show you how I felt. I don't remember exactly. But I believe it's the second Saturday after I come that when I'm at the window just before I go for my wine I feel somebody's hand on my shoulder and it's Mr Sims. He must walk very quiet because I don't know a thing till he touch me.

He says hullo, then he tells me I've got terrible thin, do I ever eat. I say of course I eat but he goes on that it doesn't suit me at all to be so thin and he'll buy some food in the village. (That's the way he talk. There's no village here. You don't get away from London so quick.)

It don't seem to me he look very well himself, but I just say bring a drink instead, as I am not hungry.

He come back with three bottles – vermouth, gin and red wine. Then he ask if the little devil who was here last smash all the glasses and I tell him she smash some, I find the pieces. But not all. 'You fight with her, eh?'

He laugh, and he don't answer. He pour out the drinks then he says, 'Now, you eat up those sandwiches.'

Some men when they are there you don't worry so much. These sort of men you do all they tell you blindfold because they can take the trouble from your heart and make you think you're safe. It's nothing they say or do. It's a feeling they can give you. So I don't talk with him seriously – I don't want to spoil that evening. But I ask about the house and why it's so empty and he says:

'Has the old trout upstairs been gossiping?'

I tell him, 'She suppose they make difficulties for you.'

'It was a damn bad buy,' he says and talks about selling the lease or something. I don't listen much.

We were standing by the window then and the sun low. No more glare. He puts his hand over my eyes. 'Too big – much too big for your face,' he says and kisses me like you kiss a baby. When he takes his hand away I see he's looking out at the garden and he says this – 'It gets you. My God it does.'

I know very well it's not me he means, so I ask him, 'Why sell it then? If you like it, keep it.'

'Sell what?' he says. 'I'm not talking about this damned house.'

I ask what he's talking about. 'Money,' he says. 'Money. That's what I'm talking about. Ways of making it.'

'I don't think so much of money. It don't like me and what do I care?' I was joking, but he turns around, his face quite pale and he tells me I'm a fool. He tells me I'll get push around all my life and die like a dog, only worse because they'd finish off a dog, but they'll let me live till I'm a caricature of myself. That's what he say, 'Caricature of yourself.' He say I'll curse the day I was born and everything and everybody in this bloody world before I'm done.

I tell him, 'No I'll never feel like that,' and he smiles, if you can call it a smile, and says he's glad I'm content with my lot. 'I'm disappointed in you, Selina. I thought you had more spirit.'

'If I contented that's all right,' I answer him, 'I don't see very many looking contented over here.' We're standing staring at each other when the door bell rings. 'That's a friend of mine,' he says. 'I'll let him in.'

As to the friend, he's all dressed up in stripe pants and a black jacket and he's carrying a brief-case. Very ordinary looking but with a soft kind of voice.

'Maurice, this is Selina Davis,' says Mr Sims, and Maurice smiles very kind but it don't mean much, then he looks at his watch and says they ought to be getting along.

At the door Mr Sims tells me he'll see me next week and I answer straight out, 'I won't be here next week because I want a job and I won't get one in this place.'

'Just what I'm going to talk about. Give it a week longer, Selina.'

I say, 'Perhaps I stay a few more days. Then I go. Perhaps I go before.'

'Oh no you won't go,' he says.

They walk to the gates quickly and drive off in a yellow car.

Then I feel eyes on me and it's the woman and her husband in the next door garden watching. The man make some remark and she look at me so hateful, so hating I shut the front door quick.

I don't want more wine. I want to go to bed early because I must think. I must think about money. It's true I don't care for it. Even when somebody steal my savings – this happen soon after I get to the Notting Hill house – I forget it soon. About thirty pounds they steal. I keep it roll up in a pair of stockings, but I go to the drawer one day, and no money. In the end I have to tell the police. They ask me exact sum and I say I don't count it lately, about thirty pounds. 'You don't know how much?' they say. 'When did you count it last? Do you remember? Was it before you move or after?'

I get confuse, and I keep saying, 'I don't remember,' though I remember well I see it two days before. They don't believe me and when a policeman come to the house I hear the landlady tell him, 'She certainly had no money when she came here. She wasn't able to pay a month's rent in advance for her room though it's a rule in this house.' 'These people terrible liars,' she say and I think 'It's you a terrible liar, because when I come you tell me weekly or monthly as you like.' It's from that time she don't speak to me and perhaps it's she take it. All I know is I never see one penny of my savings again, all I know is they pretend I never have any, but as it's gone, no use to cry about it. Then my mind goes to my father, for my father is a white man and I think a lot about him. If I could see him only once, for I too small to remember when he was there. My mother is fair coloured woman, fairer than I am they say, and she don't stay long with me either. She have a chance to go to Venezuela when I three-four year old and she never come back. She send money instead. It's my grandmother take care of me. She's quite dark and what we call 'country-cookie' but she's the best I know.

She save up all the money my mother send, she don't keep one penny for herself – that's how I get to England. I was a bit late in going to school regular, getting on for twelve years, but I can sew very beautiful, excellent – so I think I get a good job – in London perhaps.

However here they tell me all this fine handsewing take too

long. Waste of time – too slow. They want somebody to work quick and to hell with the small stitches. Altogether it don't look so good for me, I must say, and I wish I could see my father. I have his name – Davis. But my grandmother tell me, 'Every word that come out of that man's mouth a damn lie. He is certainly first class liar, though no class otherwise.' So perhaps I have not even his real name.

Last thing I see before I put the light out is the postcard on the dressing table. 'Not to worry.'

Not to worry! Next day is Sunday, and it's on the Monday the people next door complain about me to the police. That evening the woman is by the hedge, and when I pass her she says in very sweet quiet voice, '*Must* you stay? *Can't* you go?' I don't answer. I walk out in the street to get rid of her. But she run inside her house to the window, she can still see me. Then I start to sing, so she can understand I'm not afraid of her. The husband call out: 'If you don't stop that noise I'll send for the police.' I answer them quite short. I say, 'You go to hell and take your wife with you.' And I sing louder.

The police come pretty quick – two of them. Maybe they just round the corner. All I can say about police, and how they behave is I think it all depend who they dealing with. Of my own free will I don't want to mix up with police. No.

One man says, you can't cause this disturbance here. But the other asks a lot of questions. What is my name? Am I tenant of a flat in No. 17? How long have I lived there? Last address and so on. I get vexed the way he speak and I tell him, 'I come here because somebody steal my savings. Why you don't look for my money instead of bawling at me? I work hard for my money. All-you don't do one single thing to find it.'

'What's she talking about?' the first one says, and the other one tells me, 'You can't make that noise here. Get along home. You've been drinking.'

I see that woman looking at me and smiling, and other people at their windows, and I'm so angry I bawl at them too. I say, 'I have absolute and perfect right to be in the street same as anybody else, and I have absolute and perfect right to ask the police why they don't even look for my money when it disappear. It's because a dam' English thief take it you don't look,' I say. The end of all this is that I have to go before a magistrate, and he fine me five pounds for drunk and disorderly, and he give me two weeks to pay.

When I get back from the court I walk up and down the kitchen, up and down, waiting for six o'clock because I have no five pounds left, and I don't know what to do. I telephone at six and a woman answers me very short and sharp, then Mr Sims comes along and he don't sound too pleased either when I tell him what happen. 'Oh Lord!' he says, and I say I'm sorry. 'Well don't panic,' he says, 'I'll pay the fine. But look, I don't think….' Then he breaks off and talk to some other person in the room. He goes on, 'Perhaps better not stay at No. 17. I think I can arrange something else. I'll call for you Wednesday – Saturday latest. Now behave till then.' And he hang up before I can answer that I don't want to wait till Wednesday, much less Saturday. I want to get out of that house double quick and with no delay. First I think I ring back, then I think better not as he sound so vex.

I get ready, but Wednesday he don't come, and Saturday he don't come. All the week I stay in the flat. Only once I go out and arrange for bread, milk and eggs to be left at the door, and seems to me I meet up with a lot of policemen. They don't look at me, but they see me all right. I don't want to drink – I'm all the time listening, listening and thinking, how can I leave before I know if my fine is paid? I tell myself the police let me know, that's certain. But I don't trust them. What they care? The answer is Nothing. Nobody care. One afternoon I knock at the old lady's flat upstairs, because I get the idea she give me good advice. I can hear her moving about and talking, but she don't answer and I never try again.

Nearly two weeks pass like that, then I telephone. It's the woman speaking and she say, 'Mr Sims is not in London at present.' I ask, 'When will he be back – it's urgent,' and she hang up. I'm not surprised. Not at all. I knew that would happen. All the same I feel heavy like lead. Near the phone box is a chemist's shop, so I ask him for something to make me sleep, the day is bad enough, but to lie awake all night – Ah no! He gives me a little bottle marked *'One or two tablets only'* and I take three when I go to bed because more and more I thinking that sleeping is better than no matter what else. However, I lie there, eyes wide open as usual, so I take three more. Next thing I know the room is full of sunlight, so it must be late afternoon, but the lamp is still on. My head turn around and I can't think well at all. At first I ask myself how I get to the place. Then it comes to me, but in pictures – like the landlady kicking my dress, and when I take my ticket at Victoria Station, and Mr Sims telling me to eat the sandwiches, but I can't remember everything clear, and I feel very giddy and sick. I take in the milk and eggs at the door, go in the kitchen, and try to eat but the food hard to swallow.

It's when I'm putting the things away that I see the bottles – pushed back on the lowest shelf in the cupboard.

There's a lot of drink left, and I'm glad I tell you. Because I can't bear the way I feel. Not any more. I mix a gin and vermouth and I drink it quick, then I mix another and drink it slow by the window. The garden looks different, like I never see it before. I know quite well what I must do, but it's late now – tomorrow. I have one more drink, of wine this time, and then a song come in my head, I sing it and I dance it, and more I sing, more I am sure this is the best tune that has ever come to me in all my life.

The sunset light from the window is gold colour. My shoes sound loud on the boards. So I take them off, my stockings too and go on dancing but the room feel shut in, I can't breathe, and I go outside still singing. Maybe I dance a bit too. I forget all about that woman till I hear her saying, 'Henry, look at this.' I turn around and I see her at the window. 'Oh yes, I wanted to speak with you,' I say, 'Why bring the police and get me in bad trouble? Tell me that.'

'And you tell *me* what you're doing here at all,' she says. 'This is a respectable neighbourhood.'

Then the man come along. 'Now young woman, take yourself off. You ought to be ashamed of this behaviour.'

'It's disgraceful,' he says, talking to his wife, but loud so I can hear, and she speaks loud too – for once. 'At least the other tarts that crook installed here were *white* girls,' she says.

'You a dam' fouti liar,' I say. 'Plenty of those girls in your country already. Numberless as the sands on the shore. You don't need me for that.'

'You're not a howling success at it certainly.' Her voice sweet sugar again. 'And you won't be seeing much more of your friend Mr Sims. He's in trouble too. Try somewhere else. Find somebody else. If you can, of course.' When she say that my arm moves of itself. I pick up a stone and bam! through the window. Not the one they are standing at but the next, which is of coloured glass, green and purple and yellow.

I never see a woman look so surprise. Her mouth fall open she so full of surprise. I start to laugh, louder and louder – I laugh like my grandmother, with my hands on my hips and my head back. (When she laugh like that you can hear her to the end of the street.) At last I say, 'Well, I'm sorry. An accident. I get it fixed tomorrow early.' 'That glass is irreplaceable,' the man says. 'Irreplaceable.' 'Good thing,' I say, 'those colours look like they sea-sick to me. I buy you a better windowglass.'

He shake his fist at me. 'You won't be let off with a fine this time,' he says. Then they draw the curtains. I call out at them. 'You run away. Always you run away. Ever since I come here you hunt me down because I don't answer back. It's you shameless.' I try to sing 'Don't trouble me now'.

Don't trouble me now
You without honour.
Don't walk in my footstep
You without shame.

But my voice don't sound right, so I get back indoors and drink one more glass of wine – still wanting to laugh, and still thinking of my grandmother for that is one of her songs.

It's about a man whose doudou give him the go-by when she find somebody rich and he sail away to Panama. Plenty people die there of fever when they make that Panama canal so long ago. But he don't die. He come back with dollars and the girl meet him on the jetty, all dressed up and smiling. Then he sing to her, 'You without honour, you without shame.' It sound good in Martinique patois too: 'Sans honte'.

Afterwards I ask myself, 'Why I do that? It's not like me. But if they treat you wrong over and over again the hour strike when you burst out that's what.'

Too besides, Mr Sims can't tell me now I have no spirit. I don't care, I sleep quickly and I'm glad I break the woman's

ugly window. But as to my own song it go *right* away and it
never come back. A pity.

Next morning the doorbell ringing wake me up. The people
upstairs don't come down, and the bell keeps on like fury self.
So I go look, and there is a policeman and a policewoman
outside. As soon as I open the door the woman put her foot in
it. She wear sandals and thick stockings and I never see a foot
so big or so bad. It look like it want to mash up the whole
world. Then she come in after the foot, and her face not so
pretty either. The policeman tell me my fine is not paid and
people make serious complaints about me, so they're taking
me back to the magistrate. He show me a paper and I look at it,
but I don't read it. The woman push me in the bedroom, and
tell me to get dress quickly, but I just stare at her, because I
think perhaps I wake up soon. Then I ask her what I must
wear. She say she suppose I had some clothes on yesterday.
Or not? 'What's it matter, wear anything,' she says. But I find
clean underclothes and stockings and my shoes with high
heels and I comb my hair. I start to file my nails, because I think
they too long for magistrate's court but she get angry. 'Are you
coming quietly or aren't you?' she says. So I go with them and
we get in a car outside.

I wait for a long time in a room full of policemen. They come
in, they go out, they telephone, they talk in low voices. Then
it's my turn, and first thing I notice in the court room is a man
with frowning black eyebrows. He sit below the magistrate, he
dressed in black and he so handsome I can't take my eyes off
him. When he see that he frown worse than before.

First comes a policeman to testify I cause disturbance, and
then comes the old gentleman from next door. He repeat that
bit about nothing but the truth so help me God. Then he says I
make dreadful noise at night and use abominable language,
and dance in obscene fashion. He says when they try to shut
the curtains because his wife so terrify of me, I throw stones
and break a valuable stain-glass window. He say his wife get
serious injury if she'd been hit, and as it is she in terrible
nervous condition and the doctor is with her. I think, 'Believe
me, if I aim at your wife I hit your wife – that's certain.' 'There
was no provocation,' he says. 'None at all.' Then another lady
from across the street says this is true. She heard no

provocation whatsoever, and she swear that they shut the curtains but I go on insulting them and using filthy language and she saw all this and heard it.

The magistrate is a little gentleman with a quiet voice, but I'm very suspicious of these quiet voices now. He ask me why I don't pay my fine, and I say because I haven't the money. I get the idea they want to find out all about Mr Sims – they listen so very attentive. But they'll find out nothing from me. He ask how long I have the flat and I say I don't remember. I know they want to trip me up like they trip me up about my savings so I won't answer. At last he ask me if I have anything to say as I can't be allowed to go on being a nuisance. I think, 'I'm nuisance to you because I have no money that's all.' I want to speak up and tell him how they steal all my savings, so when my landlord asks for month's rent I haven't got it to give. I want to tell him the woman next door provoke me since long time and call me bad names but she have a soft sugar voice and nobody hear – that's why I broke her window, but I'm ready to buy another after all. I want to say all I do is sing in that old garden, and I want to say this in decent quiet voice. But I hear myself talking loud and I see my hands wave in the air. Too besides it's no use, they won't believe me, so I don't finish. I stop, and I feel the tears on my face. 'Prove it.' That's all they will say. They whisper, they whisper. They nod, they nod.

Next thing I'm in a car again with a different policewoman, dressed very smart. Not in uniform. I ask her where she's taking me and she says 'Holloway' just that 'Holloway'.

I catch hold of her hand because I'm afraid. But she takes it away. Cold and smooth her hand slide away and her face is china face – smooth like a doll and I think, 'This is the last time I ask anything from anybody. So help me God.'

The car come up to a black castle and little mean streets are all around it. A lorry was blocking up the castle gates. When it get by we pass through and I am in jail. First I stand in a line with others who are waiting to give up handbags and all belongings to a woman behind bars like in a post office. The girl in front bring out a nice compact, look like gold to me, lipstick to match and a wallet full of notes. The woman keep the money, but she give back the powder and lipstick and she half-smile. I have two pounds seven shillings and sixpence in pennies. She take my purse, then she throw me my compact (which is cheap) my comb and my handkerchief like everything in my bag is dirty. So I think, 'Here too, here too.' But I tell myself, 'Girl, what you expect, eh? They all like that. All.'

Some of what happen afterwards I forget, or perhaps better not remember. Seems to me they start by trying to frighten you. But they don't succeed with me for I don't care for nothing now, it's as if my heart hard like a rock and I can't feel.

Then I'm standing at the top of a staircase with a lot of women and girls. As we are going down I notice the railing very low on one side, very easy to jump, and a long way below there's the grey stone passage like it's waiting for you.

As I'm thinking this a uniform woman step up alongside quick and grab my arm. She say, 'Oh no you don't.'

I was just noticing the railing very low that's all – but what's the use of saying so.

Another long line waits for the doctor. It move forward slowly and my legs terrible tired. The girl in front is very young and she cry and cry. 'I'm scared,' she keeps saying. She's lucky in a way – as for me I never will cry again. It all dry up and hard in me now. That, and a lot besides. In the end I tell her to stop, because she doing just what these people want her to do.

She stop crying and start a long story, but while she is speaking her voice get very far away, and I find I can't see her face clear at all.

Then I'm in a chair, and one of those uniform women is pushing my head down between my knees, but let her push – everything go away from me just the same.

They put me in the hospital because the doctor say I'm sick. I have cell by myself and it's all right except I don't sleep. The things they say you mind I don't mind.

When they clang the door on me I think, 'You shut me in, but you shut all those other dam' devils *out*. They can't reach me now.'

At first it bothers me when they keep on looking at me all through the night. They open a little window in the doorway to do this. But I get used to it and get used to the night chemise they give me. It very thick, and to my mind it not very clean either – but what's that matter to me? Only the food I can't swallow – especially the porridge. The woman ask me sarcastic, 'Hunger striking?' But afterwards I can leave most of it, and she don't say nothing.

One day a nice girl comes around with books and she give me two, but I don't want to read so much. Beside one is about a murder, and the other is about a ghost and I don't think it's at all like those books tell you.

There is nothing I want now. It's no use. If they leave me in peace and quiet that's all I ask. The window is barred but not small, so I can see a little thin tree through the bars, and I like watching it.

After a week they tell me I'm better and I can go out with the others for exercise. We walk round and round one of the yards in that castle – it is fine weather and the sky is a kind of pale blue, but the yard is a terrible sad place. The sunlight fall down and die there. I get tired walking in high heels and I'm glad when that's over.

We can talk, and one day an old woman come up and ask me for dog-ends. I don't understand, and she start muttering at me like she very vexed. Another woman tell me she mean cigarette ends, so I say I don't smoke. But the old woman still look angry, and when we're going in she give me one push and I nearly fall down. I'm glad to get away from these people, and hear the door clang and take my shoes off.

Sometimes I think, 'I'm here because I wanted to sing' and I have to laugh. But there's a small looking glass in my cell and I see myself and I'm like somebody else. Like some strange new person. Mr Sims tell me I too thin, but what he say now to this person in the looking glass? So I don't laugh again.

Usually I don't think at all. Everything and everybody seem small and far away, that is the only trouble.

Twice the doctor come to see me. He don't say much and I don't say anything, because a uniform woman is always there. She look like she thinking, 'Now the lies start.' So I prefer not to speak. Then I'm sure they can't trip me up. Perhaps I there still, or in a worse place. But one day this happen.

We were walking round and round in the yard and I hear a woman singing – the voice come from high up, from one of the small barred windows. At first I don't believe it. Why should anybody sing here? Nobody want to sing in jail, nobody want to do anything. There's no reason, and you have no hope. I think I must be asleep, dreaming, but I'm awake all right and I see all the others are listening too. A nurse is with us that afternoon, not a policewoman. She stop and look up at the window.

It's a smoky kind of voice, and a bit rough sometimes, as if those old dark walls themselves are complaining, because they see too much misery – too much. But it don't fall down and die in the courtyard; seems to me it could jump the gates of the jail easy and travel far, and nobody could stop it. I don't hear the words – only the music. She sing one verse and she begin another, then she break off sudden. Everybody starts walking again, and nobody says one word. But as we go in I ask the woman in front who was singing. 'That's the Holloway song,' she says. 'Don't you know it yet? She was singing from the punishment cells, and she tell the girls cheerio and never say die.' Then I have to go one way to the hospital block and she goes another so we don't speak again.

When I'm back in my cell I can't just wait for bed. I walk up and down and I think. 'One day I hear that song on trumpets and these walls will fall and rest.' I want to get out so bad I could hammer on the door, for I know now that anything can happen, and I don't want to stay lock up here and miss it.

Then I'm hungry. I eat everything they bring and in the morning I'm still so hungry I eat the porridge. Next time the doctor come he tells me I seem much better. Then I say a little of what really happen in that house. Not much. Very careful.

He look at me hard and kind of surprised. At the door he shake his finger and says, 'Now don't let me see you here again.'

That evening the woman tells me I'm going, but she's so upset about it I don't ask questions. Very early, before it's light she bangs the door open and shouts at me to hurry up. As we're going along the passages I see the girl who gave me the books. She's in a row with others doing exercises. Up Down, Up Down, Up. We pass quite close and I notice she's looking very pale and tired. It's crazy, it's all crazy. This up down business and everything else too. When they give me my money I remember I leave my compact in the cell, so I ask if I can go back for it. You should see that policewoman's face as she shoo me on.

There's no car, there's a van and you can't see through the windows. The third time it stop I get out with one other, a young girl, and it's the same magistrates' court as before.

The two of us wait in a small room, nobody else there, and after a while the girl say, 'What the hell are they doing? I don't want to spend all day here.' She go to the bell and she keep her finger press on it. When I look at her she say, 'Well, what are they *for*?' That girl's face is hard like a board – she could change faces with many and you wouldn't know the difference. But she get results certainly. A policeman come in, all smiling, and we go in the court. The same magistrate, the same frowning man sits below, and when I hear my fine is paid I want to ask who paid it, but he yells at me. 'Silence.'

I think I will never understand the half of what happen, but they tell me I can go, and I understand that. The magistrate ask if I'm leaving the neighbourhood and I say yes, then I'm out in the streets again, and it's the same fine weather, same feeling I'm dreaming.

When I get to the house I see two men talking in the garden. The front door and the door of the flat are both open. I go in, and the bedroom is empty, nothing but the glare streaming inside because they take the Venetian blinds away. As I'm wondering where my suitcase is, and the clothes I leave in the wardrobe, there's a knock and it's the old lady from upstairs carrying my case packed, and my coat is over her arm. She says she sees me come in. 'I kept your things for you.' I start to thank her but she turn her back and walk away. They like that here, and better not expect too much. Too besides, I bet they tell her I'm terrible person.

I go in the kitchen, but when I see they are cutting down the big tree at the back I don't stay to watch.

At the station I'm waiting for the train and a woman asks if I feel well. 'You look so tired,' she says. 'Have you come a long way?' I want to answer, 'I come so far I lose myself on that journey.' But I tell her, 'Yes, I am quite well. But I can't stand the heat.' She says she can't stand it either, and we talk about the weather till the train come in.

I'm not frightened of them any more – after all what else can they do? I know what to say and everything go like a clock works.

I get a room near Victoria where the landlady accept one
pound in advance, and next day I find a job in the kitchen of a
private hotel close by. But I don't stay there long. I hear of
another job going in a big store – altering ladies' dresses and I
get that. I lie and tell them I work in very expensive New York
shop. I speak bold and smooth faced, and they never check up
on me. I make a friend there – Clarice – very light coloured,
very smart, she have a lot to do with the customers and she
laugh at some of them behind their backs. But I say it's not
their fault if the dress don't fit. Special dress for one person
only – that's very expensive in London. So it's take in, or let out
all the time. Clarice have two rooms not far from the store. She
furnish them herself gradual and she gives parties sometimes
Saturday nights. It's there I start whistling the Holloway Song.
A man comes up to me and says, 'Let's hear that again.' So I
whistle it again (I never sing now) and he tells me 'Not bad'.
Clarice have an old piano somebody give her to store and he
plays the tune, jazzing it up. I say, 'No, not like that,' but
everybody else say the way he do it is first class. Well I think no
more of this till I get a letter from him telling me he has sold the
song and as I was quite a help he encloses five pounds with
thanks.

I read the letter and I could cry. For after all, that song was all
I had. I don't belong nowhere really, and I haven't money to
buy my way to belonging. I don't want to either.

But when that girl sing, she sing to me, and she sing for me. I
was there because I was *meant* to be there. It was *meant* I should
hear it – this I *know*.

Now I've let them play it wrong, and it will go from me like
all the other songs – like everything. Nothing left for me at all.

But then I tell myself all this is foolishness. Even if they
played it on trumpets, even if they played it just right, like I
wanted – no walls would fall so soon. 'So let them call it jazz,' I
think, and let them play it wrong. That won't make no
difference to the song I heard.

I buy myself a dusty pink dress with the money.